MARK
ANCHOVY
WAR & PIZZA

MARK ANCHOVY

WAR & PIZZA

William Goldsmith

Piccadilly
PRESS

First published in Great Britain in 2021 by
PICCADILLY PRESS
An imprint of Bonnier Books UK
The Plaza, 535 King's Road, London, SW10 0SZ
Owned by Bonnier Books
Sveavägen 56, Stockholm, Sweden

Text and illustrations © William Goldsmith 2021

A CIP catalogue record for this book is available from the British Library.

ISBN: 978-1-84812-927-6
Also available as an ebook and audiobook

To Alicia

Chapter 1

My employers, the Golden Spatula League, promise their detectives both luxury and danger.

Interpreting 'luxury' as a secret office with a hot tub, I glossed over the 'danger' part. I didn't think I'd be chased by an actual wolf. Or get ejected from a plane. Or have my eyebrows singed off. Plus, there was no hot tub. If I'd known then what I know now, I might never have answered the pizza-phone when it angrily tootled one night in December.

'Yes?'

'Since when is "yes?" how you answer the phone to a superior?'

It was my boss, Princess Skewer. Skewer, because of the kebabs she sells. Princess, because she acts like one.

'I mean . . . Mark Anchovy spea–'

'Did you get the assignment?'

'Which assignment?'

I capsized the tower of light-blue envelopes sprouting from my desk. My training had recently gone from intensive to turbo. Here was a questionnaire on the league's founding (1867); here were certificates for elementary contortion, calligraphy and fencing. Here was a pamphlet titled 'How to Spot a Criminal of the Catering Underworld'.

'Anchovy. If you plan to stay in a G.S.L. job – which many would give their right arm for' – I'm left-handed, so this was lost on me – 'I suggest you get a filing system.'

She sounded just like Mr Hogstein, my crusty history teacher.

'It's okay, I've found it.'

'There's no time. Head up to Caesar Pizza. Over and out.'

No sooner had I twisted the tomato can that activated the fake door, shot up the ladder and casually strolled into my parents' pizzeria, than the main line rang.

My mum answered in her super-polite, high-pitched voice.

'Yes yes, a Mark Anchovy pizza with *extra* anchovies? Yes yes, right away.'

My dad's monobrow wiggled like a belly-dancing slug. He picked up a rolling pin and set to work.

'Odd,' said my mum, handing me the address. 'He wants it delivered to a houseboat.'

Something tugged on my apron. Something with a wonky fringe and laser-like gaze: Alicia, my sister.

'Colinnnnnnnnnnnnnnnn,' she chanted.

Sometimes I get so used to my codename, Mark Anchovy, that I blank out my less exciting real name.

'What now, Alicia?'

'Who were you talking to in the storeroom?'

'Er . . . myself.'

'Yourself?'

'Uh-huh.'

'Right. I thought you were, you know, talking to friends or practising your lines for that arty-farty school play. But you were talking to yourself?'

'Yep.'

'Weirrrrrrrdoooooooooooooooooooo!!' She climbed onto a high stool and began shredding napkins. When Alicia wasn't climbing things, she was cutting things. Like her own hair. Or family albums. Or *my* comics. And when she wasn't doing this, she was twanging a double bass, when tinkling a nice, quiet triangle would have been fine.

The cheesy, salty-fishy waft of a cooked Mark Anchovy pizza tickled my nostrils.

'No faffing,' was my dad's pearl of wisdom as he packed up the pizza.

'Is your bike light working?' fretted my mum.

Considering what lay ahead, worrying about a bike light was like questioning your choice of swimming trunks in the face of a tsunami.

Apart from a seagull maiming a bin bag, the streets were empty. I left town via the long dark gullet of Saltpan Lane. I passed the abandoned windmill, its tired sails groaning. River reeds moshed. Mud replaced tarmac. Marsh replaced mud. Finally, in the bottle-green blackness, the light of a boat bobbed up ahead. I sludged down the bank. My pizza watch beeped with instructions from Princess:

Let me know what he wants. P.S.

I drew up the collar of my trench coat – well, my mum's trench coat – and rapped on a porthole.

No answer. I heard a radio tinkling and a kettle reaching boiling point. It wasn't the only one. Dodging a scabby rope, I knocked on the cabin's hobbit-door.

'Mark Anchovy Pizza!' I scanned my mum's note. 'For a Mr . . . Swirly Ben?' Was that even a name? 'Helloooooo?'

Nothing. Apparently, we now delivered pizzas to corpses.

No one home, I typed to Princess.

Weird, she replied. **Have a quick snoop then get out.**

I heaved a sigh and opened the door. It was a narrow, coffin-like space, with a knotty pine table and a mounted lamp. Opposite this was a cuckoo clock, of all things. A saucepan was bubbling on a

dinky hob. Inside, an egg was going berserk. And
on the sideboard lay a chipped flowery plate with
fingers of toast spread like sunbeams. A boiled egg
and soldiers? *And* pizza? Was Swirly Ben some kind
of unstoppable eating machine? I went snooping.
There was a bathroom with a bucket, and a bar of
soap that looked like it would actually make you
dirtier. There was a cabinet with brown glass pill-
bottles. A bedroom with a fat fur coat on a skinny
bed. An old brick phone. A book on antiques. A
pamphlet with the title 'Baltic Cruises'. An empty,
teal-coloured
glasses case that
snapped like a
clam. A torn
sepia photograph
of some kids on a pier,
posing in smocks and
sailor suits. And a postcard

of a church, with a note in an unfamiliar alphabet. This, I pocketed. There was nothing in the way of a wallet. And nothing in the way of Swirly Ben.

Well??? beeped Princess.

I returned to the main cabin. I needed to sit – and eat – and think about all this. If there was a

newly boiled egg, a phone and a fur coat, then this hungry, loopy old antique-lover couldn't have got far. I opened the satchel and took a slice of pizza. An anchovy plopped off and I bent down to get it. But when I came up, the slice of pizza where my head had been was now a mere crust. The rest of the slice was splatted on the wall behind me in several explosive blobs. It was pinned there by an arrow.

Earth to Anchovy???!! Princess texted again with impeccable timing.

My mission in Rome taught me that when pizzas explode where your head just was, you don't reply to a text message. You duck under a table and reach for your molten-tomato-purée gun. Any worries I used to have about using this deadly weapon vanished.

Cycling along a marsh in winter, delivering a pizza, not getting a tip, being interrupted while eating, and now assassination! Who did this Swirly Ben think he was? I stuck out a hand and fired a jet of lava-like tomato. There was a *hiss* as it scorched a hole somewhere. Then a cartoonish squeak. I jutted out an eyebrow. It was the cuckoo clock. Something was winding out.

Only it wasn't a merry little wooden bird. It was some kind of mechanically powered crossbow. Pointed at *me*. I just ducked in time. *THUNK!* went the arrow. The raggedy bits of pizza took another pasting. *THUNK!* went another arrow. Pizza bits rained down. *THUNK!* went a third arrow. An olive beetled down my neck. I had to stop that clock! I slid on my belly and molten-tomatoed it from the end of the table. The good news was, it clogged up the machinery. The bad news was, the lamp exploded. It happened too fast to take everything in, but I think it sparked, and the sparks decided to bounce all over the oven. It would have been very simple to have turned off the gas when I looked in the pan. But I didn't. And we all know what happens when a spark meets a lit gas hob. They get on like a houseboat on fire. The next thing I knew was that the space – which I mentioned as being appropriately coffin-width – was filling up with smoke. Not wanting to be left out, a few tea towels had also lent themselves to the inferno.

Erm . . . message me, please???!! Princess rat-a-tatted on my watch.

Can't talk right now . . . I'm kind of being assassinated by a booby-trapped boat. I immediately regretted my lack of economy. The flames were now breakdancing in a hot orange cyclone. I got off my belly and made for the hobbit-door. But as soon as I stood up, I was flung back down. The boat was spinning. Spinning, I realised, because it was no longer tied to the bank. Which meant that this floating incinerator was in the middle of a river with only one very wet means of exit. Sometimes, on long car journeys, after she's stolen my last fruit pastille (which is always a black one) Alicia and I ask each other random questions like, 'Would you rather burn to death or freeze to death?' It now seemed I was a fan of the second option. Somehow, I charged out of the spinning cabin, didn't puke, half-dodged a wall of fire, and jumped into the river, trench coat and all. When I'd wiped the algae off my eyeballs, I watched the burning carcass slip below the surface. Whatever evidence I could have gathered about Swirly Ben was wasted. Along with a perfectly good pizza.

Chapter 2

The hall was swallowed up by a sinister blob of shadow. Mr Hogstein was on the stage.

'Item One,' he began. 'No doubt, children, you saw the hideous piece of arson on the news?'

'Piece of what, sir?!' shouted Dexter, the wedgie king.

'Arson.' Hogstein clucked like a sergeant major. 'I said *arson*, Dexter. And I see nothing funny about it. Arson is when somebody burns something *illegally*.' He swivelled his snooker-ball eyes towards me. '*Illegally*.' He held the Hog-stare. Princess could take him, I thought. But not me. I stared up at the cricket nets.

'If it transpires that any pupils from Rufflington Community School were responsible for such a crime, I can assure you that the terrible majesty of the law will –'

'Colin, is he looking at *you*?' whispered Robin, the sleepy kid next to me. I shrugged. I couldn't get those images out of my mind. The burning boat. The demented cuckoo clock. My parents' faces when they saw how wet I was, how late I was, how much I was shivering. Alicia, asking how I'd singed off my eyebrows. I could remember those images so clearly, down to every last detail, that they were starting to hurt my head. This had been happening a lot recently. It was like a memory overload.

'Item Two,' barked Hogstein. 'Thankfully, we move on to cheerier matters. The school play. Now, there have been murmurings that a stage adaptation of *War and Peace* is a trifle' – he chuckled – 'ambitious! But I have every confidence that we'll pull it off.'

This *War and Peace* job sounded like Hogstein's biggest yawnfest to date. It was going to be something like *four hours long.* I mean, where did the school find this guy? He prattled on about rehearsal times and lines to learn and wigs to source, and how we might raise money for a smoke machine by having a cake sale. I zoned out once more, until he 'Item-Three-ed' with that dramatic boom of his.

'And finally, children, the moment we've all been waiting for. The results of your applications for the school exchange programme are in. Now, I must stress, every effort was made to achieve the utmost fairness for *all* children.'

It would be easier if I explain. Basically, a number of kids learning languages had applied –

or their parents had applied – to be packed off to another country to soak up the lingo, buy a fridge magnet, and make our dud school look more international. At some point in the future, some unfortunate foreign kids would have to sit through one of our assemblies with Hogstein's bingo wings jiggling above their heads. So here it was – the day of reckoning. The list was read out. The repulsive Dexter was getting a week as a rollercoaster test-rider at Disneyland Paris. Robin, who would probably rather sleep for a week, was staying in an Alpine chalet, skiing with the family who own Nutella. Annabel would spend a week with a family of surfing instructors in Portugal. And so on. Then mine was read out.

'Colin Kingsley,' pronounced Hogstein, all magistrate-y. 'You will be going . . .'

I swear I saw a nasty smirk across his chops.

'You will be going, Kingsley . . . to Russia.'

'Sorry, sir, could you say that again? I thought you said "Russia".'

There was a victorious glimmer behind those thick glasses. 'I *did* say Russia, young man.'

There was a chorus of cackles from Dexter and his troll brigade. Some of them even high-fived. Trolls. What did I know about Russia? Not a lot, to be honest. I knew it would be snowy. And they had shiny gold onion-domes on their churches. And for some reason, I had an idea that it was just . . . well . . . a bit scary. But I don't know where that idea came from. The news? My granddad G-pops always says not to trust the news.

At break-time I came across Hogstein, hogging the photocopier, talking to Miss Odedra.

'I assure you, Kirti,' he snorted, 'it's an excellent choice: far enough away, not to mention ruddy freezing. Russia should toughen up the little bli– Oh, hello Kingsley, didn't see you there!

Excited about your little trip?'

I raised my eyebrows – what was left of them –
and strutted off. I could still hear Odedra saying
something like, 'Couldn't we just do *The Sound of
Music*, Arnold?'

The lessons thundered past me like carriages
in a freight train. My mind was elsewhere. The
houseboat. The fire. Russia. I thought about my
weird brain and why it was starting to get all these
aches whenever I remembered stuff. It's hard to
describe, but there were all these pictures, like
film stills, bouncing around in there, nipping to
the surface. And every time they did, their edges
spiked a soft part of my brain. I tried opening the
windows, sipping water, deep breaths, paracetamol.
But the images kept whirling around. And then –
just as we were learning about tectonic plates – one
image from the houseboat lodged stuck. It grew
into focus, as if under a microscope: the postcard

of the church. The strange letters on it seemed gigantic in my mind. I could imagine walking under them, as if through a doorway. They were Russian letters! Surprise, surprise – the G.S.L. had probably fiddled with the school exchange programme. They were on to something. So far, so Princess.

Chapter 3

To quote G-pops, nobody likes a hospital. There's the smell of chemicals. The smell of feet. The paper nighties they make everyone wear. The Niagara Falls sound effect of someone peeing behind a curtain. But the doctor said an MRI scan could be helpful. To explain my sudden mega-headaches. The times I felt faint and dizzy. My 'memory overloads'.

'Your son's brain is storing vast quantities of visual information, which are well above the norm,' the doctor told my parents. 'Moreover, Conrad is not simply storing these snapshots. He is being overwhelmed with them.'

'Er, his name is Colin, Dr Peatree,' my dad corrected her.

'Ah, yes. Well . . .' Dr Peabrain lowered her yellow-rimmed glasses, presumably to lend her some gravitas. 'Now it's possible that this overwhelming abundance of memory will cause problems with, say, concentration. I understand' – she lowered her voice – 'that Calvin has been having some, um, *issues* at school.'

'*Colin*,' I said slowly, staring at her constellation of freckles.

'Mr Hogstein mentioned that there's been some problems, yes,' said my mum.

'Is there a name for Colin's condition?' asked my dad.

'It's too early to tell,' said the doctor, returning to her normal voice. 'But let's see what this scan shows up. This way please, Conan.'

They strapped me to a bed which lolled like a tongue from the scanner, which resembled a giant washing machine. I had to put on these sunglasses that even my dad wouldn't wear. Finally, they strapped on a pair of chunky headphones, completing idiot mode. Buttons were punched, lights were dimmed, and the air filled with a strange hum. Slowly, the robo-washer sucked me in. I entered a big cylinder. After a minute, it began to sink . . . down, deep down, into a much darker space. There was a *CLANG*, like wheels gripping a bracket or railing. The bed lurched forward.

'Er . . . hello?' I called. 'Dr Peatree?'

I couldn't see much, as I was strapped down and wearing *those* sunglasses. But I was clearly no longer in Dr Peatree's office.

Without warning, the cylinder accelerated. Air blasted my face, stretching it like pizza dough. I felt as though I was on a track that curved in a bit here, out a bit there, like a bobsleigh ride. The wall of the cylinder flickered with occasional light. On I flew. About fifteen minutes passed before the bobsleigh-scanner began to slow. My cheeks resumed normal service. Slowly, the bed rose. A panel opened with what I felt was unnecessary violence. Daylight scorched my eyeballs. Something in the background was sizzling. Bacon?

When I'd stopped blinking, a face framed by blue-and-pink hair bobbed into the bobsleigh.

'Yelena?' I gargled, as if waking from a dream.

'Yaconda.' She sighed. 'We're not *that* similar. Aren't you supposed to have a photographic memory or something?'

'Hi, Anchovy!' A twin version of the face bobbed in.

'Yelena, Yaconda, what . . . why . . . where am I?'

'You're in a fake chest freezer in a greasy spoon café in an undisclosed street in London,' said

Yelena. She reached in and unclipped the straps.
'And you've taken the high-speed G.S.L. shuttle to
get here.'

I now saw what I'd stupidly missed earlier – the
teeny diamond of spatulas engraved on the panel.
Yelena and Yaconda were the famous impressionist
twins. They could mimic anyone. They were
forever trying on voices, like clothes in a shop.

Mostly, they used this skill for fake phone calls or diverting enemies.

'Weeeee neeeeeed to brief you,' said Yaconda, now in a hammy opera-singer voice. 'Plus Sid will come in soon for the mushy peas.'

'So best not lie there *all* day, DJ-Dad style,' added Yelena, in a Terminator voice.

I flung off the shades and headphones and sat up. We were in a stockroom that was jam-packed with eggs, crates of bread, tubs of ketchup, among other things. Yaconda nodded towards the café through the half-open door: grotty porridge-y walls with fake olde-worlde beams. From these hung a jumble of teapots, horseshoes, ugly statuettes, and grease-fogged postcards. A weeping chalkboard had been rescued from the rain. Outside, red double-deckers juddered and moaned, sloshing up the puddles. On the steamed-up window were the letters:

FRYER TUCK'S DINER

Chairs were stacked on all the tables except one. At this sat a tall girl with her back to me. She wore a long pinstriped coat, boots that meant business, and a ponytail shaped like a pirate's hook on top of her head. I went and sat opposite.

'Princess Skewer,' I said in a hushed tone.

'Well, if it isn't Mark I-make-the-rules-up-as-I-go-along Anchovy.'

'What do you mean?'

'I'll get on to that. What happened to your eyebrows?'

'I was boiling an egg . . .'

'Weird. I wanted to talk to you about boiled eggs.'

She clicked her fingers and held out her hand. A parrot-faced boy hopped up, walking as if he had a wedgie, and passed her a breakfast roll.

'Please study the menu.'

'My tummy is actually really full, Princess, tha–'

'I didn't ask you about the contents of your fluffing stomach. I asked you to study the menu.'

I opened the laminated tome.

'Tell me, Anchovy: what does the name "Brillerge" mean to you?'

'Sounds like a brand of toilet cleaner.'

'Have a look at the specials page.'

The description, in neon-yellow bubble writing, was for a greasy-as-hell fried breakfast. The picture though, showed something very different.

'Anchovy. You are looking at what we in the business refer to as "a Brillerge creation".'

Princess held up her cup and wedgie-boy poured some coffee.

'M. Brillerge was personal jeweller to the Russian royal family – before they were booted off the throne in 1917. He was the creator of some of the priciest eggs in existence.'

'Eggs?'

'Eggs. Guilloche-enamelled, solid gold-plated, jewel-studded eggs. A Brillerge egg might burn a hole in your pocket to the tune of, say, 50 million GBP, should you be carrying that kind of cashew. People who own them tend to also own small countries, oil companies or football teams.'

She mauled the breakfast roll and came up for air.

'Most famous of all are the Brillerge egg *cups*: blingtastic holders that open up to house an actual boiled egg, with mechanical arms for dunking soldiers. Only four were ever made, and they have been missing for over a century. Until now.'

'Where are these blingtastic egg cups?'

'Russia.'

'Any more info than just "Russia"? Last time I checked, Russia was pretty gigantic.'

'Only one person knows *exactly* where they are . . .' She leaned in and dolloped brown sauce all over my mum's trench coat. 'Swirly Ben.'

'You mean . . .'

'Yes. The same Swirly Ben who invited you to his houseboat. Which you then decided to torch.'

'Princess – it was booby-trapped! It set *itself* on fire!'

She sighed and downed her coffee. 'Turn to the Jacket Potatoes, please.'

Above the option **Jacket Pot with Coleslaw + Beans + Cheese** was a photo of a man with a white curtain of beard, a red beret, and a face like a turkey's saggy bits. I couldn't think who he reminded me of.

'Is this Swirly Ben?'

'Yep. He's 108 years old and he needs our help. Because right now, every jewellery thief in town has him on their hit list. Including Heidi Hyde High.'

'Who's that?'

'The nastiest jewellery thief of them all. Hot Beverages.'

Heidi Hyde High's photo was above **Hot Chocolate with a Wafer, Whipped Cream + Marshmallows**. At first I wondered if the printer had malfunctioned. Her level of spray-tan hurt the eye, as did her blinding smile, triangular eyebrows, sunglasses and little-girl pigtails. She wore black ribbons in them, like a Victorian child attending a funeral. A white fur coat topped it all off.

'She's been arrested three times,' explained Princess. 'But she always worms her way out of it. She's a former Olympic fencer and fashion model,

and currently runs an empire of caviar emporiums
across Europe.'

'Nice work if you can get it.'

'Then there's her henchman, Unkle Pudders.
Pie section.'

Above **Steak and Kidney** leered
a leathery face, with a droopy
moustache and even droopier
mouth.

'You'll be on the same flight to
Russia as Heidi Hyde High.'

'And what do you want me to do?'

'Stop her.'

'Anything else?'

'Well, return the Brillerge egg cups to their
rightful owner, of course.'

'Who is . . .?'

'Dessert menu.'

Above **Steamed Golden Syrup Sponge with**

Custard was a boy in a black waistcoat, with black hair and black rings under nervous, squirrelly eyes.

'His name is Kirill Kitov. The Brillerge egg cups belonged to his great-great-great-grandfather, but were lost in the Russian Revolution. Ask Mr Hogstein about that.'

'How am I going to meet this Kirill the Squirrel?'

'We've pulled a few strings and landed him as your school exchange buddy. You'll be staying with him and his family in St Petersburg. You'll still need to write a school report or something for Hogstein. Oh, can you pass me the salt, please?'

'But you've already finished your breakfast roll . . .'

'Who said anything about a breakfast roll?'

Sometimes it was pointless to question Princess. As I grabbed the shaker, there was an odd mechanical whirring, and our table sank down a level. We were in a vaulted corridor with plum-coloured carpets. We got out and a familiar face zoomed into view: an Italian boy with a runny nose and hair like an ink splodge.

'Camillo!'

'Anchovy!'

Camillo was an inventor. He built helicopters and motorised wheelie bins, and, I'm guessing, MRI-scanner-shuttle trains. It was his molten-tomato-purée gun that saved me on the boat.

'Morning, Cam,' said Princess. 'We're here to see the lab.'

Camillo took us down the corridor. Mounted on the walls were portraits of former G.S.L. presidents. I caught sight of my old mentor, Master Key, a dapper sushi chef. It was Master

Key who had recruited me – but he left so abruptly, without leaving a trace or even a warning. He just said that Princess Skewer would be taking up the post. She was a good boss, really. I guess there are worse things to be called than 'pizza-head' or 'son of a kebab'.

We entered the labs and passed a succession of workbenches, where children were building, drawing, test-flying, crash-landing. Like Camillo, they wore white coats over food-related uniforms: from bakeries, chocolatiers, fishmongers, sushi chains, and more. When they saw Camillo, they put down their inventions and slapped him on the back or ruffled his hair. When they saw Princess, they tried to look busy. There were hundreds of wooden drawers, with labels like 'robot fingers' or 'hairnet gas masks' or 'lemon bomb-bombs'. Camillo delved into a drawer. Then he grabbed the sleeve of my mum's trench coat, and without asking, ripped off the buttons!

'You'll need these for Russia, Anchovy.'

He then threaded a tiny fish through the buttonholes, like the wooden toggles on duffel coats.

'Glue-gun cufflinks,' he explained, and held out my arm. He twisted the tail of the fish, which vomited a jet of paste onto the wall. Camillo pressed a pencil into the paste blob. It froze rigidly to the spot.

'Good to squirt on an enemy if you want to make them stuck.'

'How are you going to get that pencil off the wall, Cam?' asked Princess.

Camillo shrugged, then handed me a mini pencil and a notepad the size of a custard cream. Weirdly, it smelt like a custard cream, too.

'Edible pencil and paper,' said Camillo. 'If you need to destroy important information. It will dissolve easily in your digestive system, unlike real pencils and paper.'

I gave it a lick. Very custard-creamy.

'Plus here is a Russian phrase book. This one you cannot eat.'

Camillo whipped off my cap and replaced it with something fluffier.

'This is your G.S.L.-issue Russian hat. It contains an oxygen mask when you pull this.' He folded down a front flap. 'And there is also a miniature snorkel inside. It is important if you are trapped in a small space or underwater or something like this.'

'Okay . . .'

'Also, you will need to learn how to drive the new –'

RIIIINNNNGG! RIINNGGG!

Princess brought out something that looked like a kebab but sounded like a telephone.

'Hello? Oh. Uh-huh. Uh-huh. What?!!' Her big dark eyes darted back and forth. Her ponytail swished like a lion's tail. She put down the kebab and paused.

'Justin's escaped.'

There's always a mole. An informer, I mean, not the skin thing or the underground animal. There's always a nasty little snitch, in other words. Ours was Justin, AKA Juice Box. A whiny apprentice who turned sour in Rome and joined the dark side. We thought he was safe and secure in a juvenile detention centre. We thought wrong.

Chapter 4

Sisters are masters of torture. Alicia could've chosen any moment to dig up the dirt on me. But she chose the exact second I got into the old Volvo, outside Caesar Pizza, ready to leave for the airport. My dad was struggling with the engine's hacking cough. From the kerb, Alicia's blonde head peeked above the window. She rapped on the glass. I rolled it down, as I thought she might have some touching goodbye. Instead she waved something at me. An envelope. Light blue, G.S.L.-stamped, *ripped open*.

'Forgot to give you this, Col,' she said. 'Arrived

while you were having that weirdly long MRI scan.'

She giggled at my worried face – which must have been expressive even without eyebrows.

'I'm sooooo sorry, Col, but I sort of accidentally opened it.'

I lunged to grab it, but was foiled by her Jedi reactions.

'Interesting title, this pamphlet.'

The blood drained from my face. My armpits had transformed into Lake Titicacas.

'Alicia . . .' I choked. 'Give. That. Back. Now.'

'Ahem.' She glanced at my dad, who was grunting at the ignition. 'An elementary guide to jewellery theft by . . .' She frowned. 'The G.S.L.'

'GIVE IT BACK!'

'Give me three reasons why.'

'Because . . . because . . . because.'

'Ah, there we go!' said my dad, finally revving up.

'This will make fascinating reading for M and D.' Alicia smirked. 'Unless . . .'

'Run inside, angel,' my dad called to Alicia. 'We're off!'

The car spluttered to life, and before I could catch what she said, we were chuntering up Brayne Road, away from Caesar Pizza, away from my secret office, with my little sister clutching *that* document.

I hated the wait before take-off. The staff were very smart on this Russian plane, with their sharp red hats, neat white gloves and gold-trimmed badges. One steward wore an eye patch – also red with a gold trim.

I felt goose bumps. Was the air-con turned to freezing? Right on cue, harsh silvery light flashed through the cabin. This was followed by a screech:

'SELFIE TIME, GWITTERPUFF!!'

There she was, like a column of smoke, towering above the crew. Heidi Hyde High. Her arm shot out, holding a diamond-encrusted phone, selfie-ing away.

'Oh, darlings! Oooooh, were you all waiting for me before you could take off, darlings? Oh, I *am* sorry – but there was some fan-*tastic* Dior in duty-free and I just had to – *I beg your pardon*, darling? What do you mean, *no dogs*? Little Gwitterpuffles *always* travels with me, don't you?'

A low growl began. I began to wonder just how 'little' this Glitterpuff was.

RRRRRRRRRR . . .

'What's that, darling? Documents? Documents! Do you know who I *am*, darling? Shall we ask Glitterpuff what he thinks about this persecution?' The angry queen bee voice melted to a soft coo.

'What do yooooou think, my wittle

Gwitterpuffles? What do you think of this mean little man with his silly little rules?'

The growling jumped up a decibel.

RRRRRRRRRRRRRRRRRRRRRR!

'What's that, Glitterpuff? You think those trousers look tasty, do you? Well, there's nothing to stop you, darling, why don't you –'

RRRRRRRRRRRRRRRRRRRR!

I nearly fell off my seat. Because what had just padded into view could scarcely be called a dog. It was more like the love child of an extra-large polar bear and a wolf on steroids. Ugly sounds then crashed together. The yelp of an air steward. The gasp of two hundred passengers. Then the *chomp chomp chomp* as the animal bred to hunt velociraptors enjoyed a bite of trouser. Then some pathetic, toadying noises.

'Oh, what's that, darling? You think there might be room after all? Oh, how *darling* of you, darling, how *divine*. Do you think you could make it *business class*, darling? Glitterpuffles does soooo love his champagne. Yes, yes. Of course, darling. Apology accepted. That would be lovely. Thank you so much, darling. Come on, Glitterpuff, we *must* get a selfie in business class . . .'

The passengers craned their heads to look at this diamond-encrusted dictator. I just caught a glimpse, before the curtain twitched, of the monstrous fur coat, the swinging pigtails and the mutant mutt padding up the aisle.

My head was spinning. I barely noticed the safety demonstration. (It had nothing about protection against wolves.) I barely noticed the take-off, the journey over lilac-puffed clouds, the peachy sun dipping on fingers of land and estuary below. The hours slipped by. In business class, more selfie-lightning flashed behind the curtains.

Then:

'Oh, what *is* it, Glitterpuffy-puff? What's that? You'd like to go for walkies? Hold on, precious . . . oh . . . yoo-hoo! You there! Could you be a darling? Glitterpuffles here wants to go for a little walkie down the aisle. Thank you, darling.'

The air steward (now rocking the ripped-trousers look) pulled back the curtains. A tangerine fist swung over the armrest. It was holding one of those stretch leads – diamond-studded, of course – which was attached to Wolf-zilla. Who began to prowl down the aisle towards us muggles in economy class. Everyone Glitterpuff passed he growled at before moving on and growling again. Prowl and growl. Prowl and growl. When his anvil-sized head came to me, he cranked it up a notch.

RARRR! RARRR! RARRR!
RARRR! RARRR! RARRR! RARRR!

I tried to look away from his bristling fur. From

his gas-flame eyes. The pendulum of drool. The collar dripping with diamonds. The lead was at full stretch – otherwise Glitterpuff would have chomped me a new pair of hot pants.

'Ooooh, what *is* it, Glitterpuff??' came the screech.

I had only one thought. I typed on my pizza watch:

Er . . . HELP??

Under control, Anch, came the reply.

No sooner had I read it when a food trolley swung out of nowhere, clonked the dog-wolf in the chops and blocked its path. I looked up. It was the air steward with the eye patch. She passed me a wet wipe.

'Chicken or fish?' she said. Then, in a lower voice, 'And please, you must take the fish, please.'

Well, I was called Anchovy. G.S.L. code, no doubt.

And sure enough, the tinfoil covering bore the diamond of spatulas.

'Also, please, take your rucksack,' the steward whispered. I slung it on. She flicked what I hoped was a sedative-laced doggy chew to Glitterpuff. He lumbered back to business class.

'What is the *matter*, Gwitterpuffles?' called Heidi.

I chuckled to myself. The old *apprentice* caterer detective would be pretty puzzled by all this. But now, as a full-on *official* caterer detective, very few things surprised me about the G.S.L.'s elaborate methods.

Now, if there's ever a dumb thing to say as a detective, caterer or otherwise, it's 'nothing surprises me'. I don't know if the fish passing through my digestive system had been farmed in a sewer but, if the sinister gurgling from my bottom was anything to go by, I wouldn't mind taking an educated guess. A seatbelt shod, a sleeping granny leapfrogged, a mad dash down the aisle, and I was in the toilet, dropping – as I've heard Dexter sneer – the kids off at the pool. The next few minutes were quite honestly the most horrific of my short career. All I can say is, I was glad I wiped. Because without warning, a mechanical arm shot from the ceiling and clamped on my head. Then, much more ominously, a seatbelt shot out and strapped me to the toilet. A mosquito-like burble from the pizza watch announced a video call from Princess.

'Anchovy. Don't be alarmed. I'm 99% sure we've got clearance on this.'

'What's on my head?'

'It's a helmet. Now, open the towel dispenser, please.'

My assignment in Rome taught me that asking questions often slowed things down.

I opened the towel dispenser. There were no

towels inside, only a pair of goggles.

'Put them on.'

Great.

'Press the flush button.'

'What's this going to do?'

'Get rid of the smell for a start.'

I flushed. There was the horrible whooshing sound you only get on plane toilets, like a deranged camel sucking the last bit of slurpie through a broken straw.

'Did you put a laxative in my meal?'

'We needed to get you out of there. Now, please press the lever on the soap dispenser.'

'But there's nothing inside,' I said, resenting this lecture on personal hygiene.

Of course, I had no time to be resentful. When I pumped the lever, the whole toilet began to shake. More than just a ladies-and-gentlemen-we're-in-an-area-of-turbulence kind of shaking. It was like being inside a cement mixer.

'Perhaps I should explain, Anchovy.'

'Yes. I really, really think you should.'

'This is a flying toilet.'

And with that, I was no longer inside the comfort of a jumbo jet but floating in the sky, on – yes, *a toilet*. Wind was whipping me like there was no tomorrow. I've never screamed so loud. Or so high-pitched.

'Keep calm, Anchovy, it's remote-controlled. We call it the Hoverbog.'

The toilet made a tinny buzz as a propeller rose up from the septic tank. I plummeted downwards, with something resembling a sense of direction. There was my first impression of Russia: fir trees in the twilight, sagging with snow.

'Why couldn't you do this on a mini-plane?' I shouted. 'Why a toilet?'

'Speak up! It's windy where you are.'

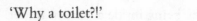

'Why a toilet?!'

'Whaaaaat?'

'WHY A TOILET?'

'I thought it would be quite handy – you know, in case you got scared and needed to go somewhere. I don't want you soiling yourself, Anchovy.'

I zipped closer to the land.

'At the same time,' she continued, 'we can't keep bailing you out like this. You're not an apprentice any more.'

Ouch. I gritted my teeth and studied the scenery. The forests turned into motorway, which gave way to giant chimneys, red and white, marbling smoke. Then tower blocks marching in lines, then the sheen of canals, crumbling pastel buildings, here a gleaming dome, there a golden spike. And closer, closer, tugboats on the ice, a paper-white park, a statue of a bald man with a goatee beard, an apartment block, a courtyard, bins, swings . . . Lower, faster, until *POP* went my parachute and my limbs jerked out. I was dangling from a tree. I unfastened my seatbelt. The toilet crashed onto a bench.

'When you cut yourself free,' said Princess, as calmly as if I had taken the bus, 'Kirill's address is block 7, fifth floor, apartment 251.'

'Right. I'm fine by the way.'

To think that once upon a time I'd actually fancied this girl!

'Oh, and Anchovy?'

'What now?'

'It isn't officially written that you should pull up your pants and trousers in order to work here, but it would be appreciated.'

Chapter 5

Piano keys were doggedly plodding inside 251. Kirill the Squirrel answered the door. He was taller than I expected, with lopsided shoulders, a jet-black swoosh of hair, and big clown feet that kept on tapping.

'Colin!' he said cheerfully and held out his hand. '*Ochen pri-yatna!*'

'*Oh-chin-pea-acne.*'

'How was your flight?'

'It was . . . exciting.'

'What happened to your suitcase?'

'Er . . . it's delayed.'

'And you are early? I was going to meet you at the airport.'

'Erm . . . it was a very speedy plane.'

'Ah. Also, you look different from your photograph,' he said.

'Yeah. I used to have eyebrows.'

He gave me slippers, then plugged some electric warmers into my trainers. It was a cosy old flat, with zig-zag floorboards, meandering plants, a hefty cabinet piled with paper, a red radio and a glass mug of tea. In the main room was a piano, a poster of a hockey team, and a sofa with a bunk bed above it.

'Are your parents here?'

Kirill fidgeted with a gold neckchain beneath his shirt.

'My father is on a trip to Moscow.'

'When is he back?'

'He was supposed to be back tonight.'

'Oh. Has he not sent you any news?'

He shrugged.

'Maybe he missed the train and will take one tomorrow morning . . .' He fidgeted again with his chain. I was going to ask more, but the *whooooosh* of something boiling made him dart into the kitchen.

'Are you hungry, Colin?'

After the plunge on the Hoverbog, I had worked up quite an appetite.

'I am making borscht for you,' Kirill said. 'Classic Russian dish.'

He kept on tapping and fidgeting. With his necklace, with his hair, with cooking utensils, the cupboard doors. Everything. From the way he was beating the wooden spoons on the bread bin, the colander and the dish rack, it was obvious he should've been a drummer, not a pianist. Maybe he could form an annoying jazz band with Alicia and her double bass. He finished his kitchen drum solo and I asked him about St Petersburg. He asked about Rufflington. I asked him if he had a history teacher as crusty as mine. He did. His father was a concert pianist. He told Kirill he should practise the piano every day. He didn't. He had never met his mum. He would turn fifteen in February.

Kirill ladled out a scarlet-coloured soup then blobbed some cream and herbs on it. We gobbled it up with bread. I said I'd try and make a Mark Anchovy pizza in return one day. Then he brought another tray from the oven. On this were golden flat-cakes, a sweet cheese curd inside.

'*Seer-niki*,' he said. 'Another classic dish.'

'Sir Nicky,' I tried.

These came with more cream, jam and mint. Then tea. (A teaspoon was also a drumstick for this kid.)

'*Spaseeba*,' I said, consulting Camillo's non-edible phrase book.

I showed Kirill my postcard of the church, salvaged from the houseboat.

'Do you know what this writing means?'

'It says . . .' He looked baffled. 'It says: "of eggs and dogs beware, beware . . . a snail and fish will meet in secret there". Where did you get this?'

'Er . . . work,' I said. *Eggs* = Brillerge. *Dogs* = Glitterpuff. *Fish* = Me? Anchovy? But a *snail*?

'Did you say a snail, Kirill?'

'Well, it says *ulitka*. Which in Russian can mean snail – or also, if you prefer, a snail-shaped pastry.'

I smiled. 'You mean like a swirly bun?'

'Yes. Like this.'

I just hoped I'd get to Swirly Ben before Heidi and the hellhound did.

'Where's the church?'

'We can go there tomorrow. It's called the Church of the Spilled Blood.'

Cheerful name. After we washed up, Kirill

practised the piano and I unpacked. My phone had taken a good spamming from Alicia.

Oh heyyyyyy Col. Doing a cheeky bit of jewellery theft out there? Message me if you want to strike a sweet deal 🖤🖤💬😋💰💰💰💰

I tackled the blackmailer.

What do you want?

The response was instant.

Sooooo I've been thinking. I CAN keep
quiet about this jewel-thieving pamphlet . . . if
IN RETURN you can:

1) Scrub out the fat in the pizza oven
   instead of me EVER doing it.

2) Pick the sweetcorn out of the
   dishwasher.

3) Do all the dog-walking and poo-bagging
   for Dinnergloves when we visit G-pops.

4) Provide me with a lifetime supply of
   black fruit pastilles.

5) Provide me with a lifetime supply of
   Oreo ice cream.

6) Never take the front seat in the car.

7) Compliment my double bass playing
   skillz.

I'll add more to this list when I have time
but at the moment I'm well busy. Let me know.
Otherwise I'm TELLING.

The worrying thing was that she was probably just getting started. I stared out the window, racking my brains. To keep her at bay, I wrote: **I'll think about it**. That was a ton of fruit pastilles to source.

Night was drawing in. A light snow whirled around the rooftops. Kirill lent me a toothbrush and a pair of pyjamas that could have doubled up as a circus tent. Then he unfolded the sofa into a bed and gave me the top bunk.

'*Spakoynee nochee*, Colin.'

'*Spark-on-knee itchy*, Kirill.'

I was guessing that meant 'good night' or 'sleep well'. If only I could. Kirill's feet thudding on the arm rest didn't help. Neither did the branches rattling against the window. Then there were the voices upstairs. As well as the clicking, like boots on a ladder. After what felt like an age, I drifted off. I saw the shrinking plane ejecting me into the

sky. I saw the rush of clouds, the canals, the parks
and the statue, crashing into close-up. Except I
landed not in the tree but in my secret office. I
cut off my parachute and realised I was tiny, and
the office was gigantic. And I couldn't reach the
tomato can that activated the door, which was
open. I climbed towards it, the clicking of boots
growing louder. And the picture of the tomato on
the can grew bigger until I saw it had eyes, staring
through the curtains at me on my top bunk. I tried
to scream, but couldn't. I felt under my pillow for
my purée gun and fired at the giant tomato in the
window. There was a burning sound. Kirill was
snoring. Was I going mad? I slid down and opened
the curtains. There was no giant tomato head.
Of course there wasn't. There were just the flats
opposite, the snow, the dancing branches. But there
remained the faint echo of boots, clicking down a
ladder.

Chapter 6

'olin,' said Kirill the next morning, 'tell me, please, why is there a big hole and some tomato ketchup on the curtains?'

I shrugged. My mind was elsewhere. It seemed my time in St Petersburg was over before it had even begun. I say this because my inbox contained this floater from Hogstein:

Good morning, Colin.

At least he kicked off with a pleasantry. It went downhill from there.

I had hoped I would never have to write these words, but it seems we have reached the final straw. I have just been paid a visit by Superintendent Sandpip from Rufflington police station. Incriminating evidence points to your involvement in the horrific houseboat fire. An anonymous witness – a young child from a different school – has testified to your delivering a pizza to the scene, moments before it was set ablaze.

What?????!!!!!!!!!!

Bizarrely, I have been unable to reach your parents.

(Had Camillo hacked the line?)

In all honesty, young man, this latest outrage comes as no surprise. Here at Rufflington Community School we all remember your *scandalous* behaviour in Rome. There, as I recall, you set off a fire alarm at an art gallery within the Vatican.

(True, but it was the only way I could access the archives for some vital info.)

Then you decided to abandon your group in the Colosseum, almost missing the bus back to the hotel.

(It was either that or get shredded by a couple of henchmen with spears, but, whatever.)

You later vandalised this bus with some libellous graffiti.

(a) It was the henchmen, not me, and (b) *libellous*?

And worst of all, you got yourself arrested by an Italian policeman, after which you had the audacity to break out of the local police cell.

Again, it was either that or get done in by the henchmen, this time armed with police truncheons. Just saying.

Thus, you leave me with no choice but to come to Russia in person to escort you back to Rufflington.

What?!! Hogstein? Coming *here*?!

I hope you realise what an astounding inconvenience this is to me, given my lead role in the school production of *War and Peace* this week, not to mention the catastrophic impact my trip will have on the school budget.

Surely the play had already done the damage to the school budget?

Since time is of the essence, I am writing this from Heathrow Airport. I shall arrive late this evening. To say I am disappointed is to understate the matter in the extreme. Your time at Rufflington Community School is almost certainly at an end. I have made recommendations for your parents to enquire into alternative educational establishments. Hopefully where your propensity for crime may be sufficiently curbed.

There weren't enough hours in the day to fire all of this through a dictionary, but I got the gist.

I shall call for you in the morning, Kingsley. I

expect you to be packed and ready to depart your poor host family. Additionally, please consider your involvement in the school play officially terminated.

Some good news at last.

Yours sincerely,

Mr Hogstein

Kirill tried to revive me with a plate of Sir Nickys.

'*Preeatnava apetita*, Colin! Do you want to see the Church of the Spilled Blood later?'

'I guess so,' I mumbled, miles away.

The Sir Nickys helped.

'Have you heard from your dad?' I asked between mouthfuls.

Kirill fiddled with his chain, as something like a gulp slid down his throat.

'No.'

We coated and booted and headed into town.

★

It was the ideal selfie spot for a jewel-nabbing maniac. Or for anyone, come to think of it. Here was the postcard picture of Russia: a gingerbread church with Christmas bauble domes. It was like someone had sat on the remote and cranked up colour mode. As stunning as it was, it was called the Church of the Spilled Blood for a reason. Someone had lobbed a bomb at the king here. Or the 'tsar', as they called them in Russia. Which sounds a lot like 'star'. And if you call yourself 'star', you're probably asking for trouble. Not that I can put that on Hogstein's worksheet. There was a nails-on-chalkboard sound of workers scraping snow, and the hiss and snap of a thousand cameras. We filed in. The first thing that shook me was the moaning. Low and pained, it rumbled in waves: a choir, chanting. All was gold, with clouds of candlelight and endless painted saints, frowning as if to say *watch out, Anchovy.* I scanned the crowds. Lots of women in shawls, crossing themselves and kissing the ikons. Lots of Japanese groups, admiring the architecture. Lots of Americans and Australians and Brits mouthing 'wow'. But no decrepit old man with a wizard-y beard and trademark red beret. Kirill went to an ikon of an angel with a sword and lit a candle. I edged up to the altar. Then something shuffled out from behind a screen: a priest, with a floor-length robe and practically floor-length beard. He slid onto a bench. I hovered, unsure. At worst, I'd get a rollicking from a Russian priest. At best, I'd get some info on some very special egg cups.

Although the air was hazy with incense, I recognised his face from Fryer Tuck's menu. Those sad, swimming eyes, magnified behind his glasses. I sat alongside him.

'Swirly Ben?'

Without answering, he handed me an enormous fur coat. I patted it, but there was nothing in the

pockets. Nothing hidden in the lining. Not even a
secret message stitched into the laundry label.

'What about the Brillerge?' I whispered.

His sad liquid eyes stared at me for a moment.
Then a voice warbled from the beard:

'Find the winter palace,

Shed the fleece and leave behind.

Take a number always moving,

The diamond's top is last in line.'

First the riddle about the snail and the fish, and
now this! Remembering that he was extremely old
and might not know where all his marbles were, I
persevered.

'The Brillerge, Mr Ben?'

At this he stood up, placed a finger over his
quivering lips, and slipped off into the candlelight,
the crowds, the wailing choir, and out of sight,
leaving me with a headache and an oversized coat.
I bundled said coat into my rucksack and pondered.

The winter palace? Shed the fleece? The diamond's top? A number always moving? That last one, I thought, as I glanced at my pizza watch, could be a reference to a clock. But that was just a hunch.

The queue for the church had doubled when we left. And elbowing through it was a moustachioed man with the physique of a potato sack. His scratchy bellow split the air.

'Outta me way!'

I recognised him from the Fryer Tuck's menu: Unkle Pudders, Heidi's henchman. No doubt he was making a beeline for a certain priest. Or, more worryingly, me. Bewildering Kirill, I wrenched open the rucksack and engulfed myself in the fur coat. It was like wearing a great big shaggy tent.

'Good coat,' said Kirill as Pudders advanced.

'Thanks,' I whispered. 'Just thought I'd pack a spare.'

I was a bad liar. But on the plus side, I was now

practically invisible to fuzzy-faced henchmen.

'Kirill,' I asked, hurrying us away and drawing up the collar, 'is there a winter palace here?'

He cocked his head to one side.

'There *was*, before the Revolution. It was where the tsar used to live, some of the time.'

'Used to?'

'This is a very long story, Colin.'

I really did need to ask Hogstein about this Russian Revolution.

'Anyway,' continued Kirill, 'now the palace is a world-famous art museum called the Hermitage. We can go there, if you like.'

We ambled along a canal, passing those cut-out boards where you stick your head through to look like you're wearing a funny outfit. I kept checking back for a potatoey henchman. I couldn't see him. There were just pastel artists making smeary caricatures, and people in felt suits, dressed as cuddly animals, or with giant vegetable-heads, handing out flyers for restaurants. We turned onto a heaving main road as a light snow began to scatter. Souvenirs gleamed in the shop windows: Russian dolls painted to look like footballers or cosmonauts or weirdly warped Simpsons; miniature Churches of the Spilled Blood; a goat made out of bread. And weirdly, key rings and fridge magnets of the Brillerge eggs.

'Do you know,' said Kirill as I gawped at them, 'we had four Brillerge egg *cups* in our family. But they went missing.'

'When was that?' I asked innocently.

'Oh, I think it was a hundred years back,' said Kirill.

'Is there any Brillerge in this palace that's no longer a palace?'

Kirill pondered, fiddling with his chain between his lips.

'Maybe.'

'Or,' I said, thinking of the riddle, 'a special clock?'

He snorted as we scuttled around some people posing as statues, spray-painted silver, then under a massive arch.

'That,' Kirill said, 'will be like finding a needle in a haystack.'

(Our parents sometimes say this about the bedroom Alicia and I share, when I'm trying to find my school tie.)

When we entered the square, I saw what he meant. The Hermitage seemed to take up the entire horizon. Mile upon mile of mint-green, gold-frilled, column-bordered rooms – it looked like the size of a small country. You probably could fit Luxembourg in there. And about a trillion clocks. Needles. Haystacks.

Once we had bought tickets, dumped our coats,

got a plastic tag, been to the loo and elbowed our way through the forest of selfie sticks, I had to stop to pick my jaw off the floor. I had never ever imagined that anywhere could be so . . . *bling-sational*. It was like the architect had been instructed by a kid with a bottomless pit of cash. *I want gold everywhere!* I could imagine them saying. *Now times that by ten! Times that by ten again! And again! Again!* But there was no time to stop and admire it. A delirious old beard (with a man attached to it) had possibly stashed some jewelled egg cups here. We had to find out where, and we had to find out now. I chivvied us up the never-ending staircase, still paranoid and on the lookout for the henchman who couldn't spell 'Uncle'. We were in there for about four hours. Ballrooms, banquet rooms, boudoirs, thrones, suits of armour, so many paintings my head began to hurt, and of course, a ton of clocks: tall, small, skinny, squat, one even shaped like a golden peacock. I peered closely at each one, looking for a switch or mechanism, a clue about the Brillerge egg cups. Nothing. To be honest, I didn't understand how all the visitors were getting through this cultural assault course. Kirill zipped around with all the energy of a pixie in a Haribo factory. I didn't have the stamina. I finally lolled onto a bench to rest my palaced-out brain. But there is some invisible force field that refuses Colin Kingsley, AKA Mark Anchovy, to have anything even resembling a rest. Alicia had texted. And dropped this:

Looks like we might need to update that list of favours, Col.

Why? I typed, less in the mood than ever.

Because I was down in the stockroom and fiddling around with the cans of chopped toms and guess what?

Oh no, I thought.

I found the magic switch

Please, no.

and stumbled upon this ol' treasure trove . . .

The ground beneath me seemed to collapse.
She'd sent me a photo of my secret office.

Could be WELL interesting for M and D, no?

My fingers flew into a furious reply.

GET OUT!!!!!!!!!!!!!!!!!!!!!!!!!!!

'Why are you looking so worried, Colin?' Kirill
had strolled over.

All I could muster was a stunned shrug. Alicia
had found my secret Colin-Cave. Which meant
she would read my G.S.L. files. Which meant
my parents would read my G.S.L. files. And this
would surely mean no G.S.L. missions. No G.S.L.
banquets. And certainly no G.S.L. hot tub, if it
ever arrived. We staggered to the exit. In the lift I
closed my eyes, trying to think. But just when you
feel you've had it all, there's always an extra dollop

of drama waiting for you to slip on. Because now there was a click-clacking. A panting. A tutting. It sounded an awful lot like someone in high heels. With a dog. We spun around.

'Oh hellooooo, darlings!'

The lift was small, but Heidi Hyde High filled it to such an extent that I actually felt like I was *inside* her fur coat. Glitterpuff was mean enough to start licking his lips.

'Do you know, darling, you're *just* the boy I wanted to see.'

Her tangerine claw lashed out. But she wasn't going for me. She was going for Kirill! In a flash she had him pinned to the wall, lifting him like a ragdoll. As I tried to get between them, Glitterpuff snarled, his horrible hackles rising. I backed into the corner, against the wall of the lift. There was a repulsive dampness as some wolf drool poured onto my sock.

'*Shto* . . . *Shto* . . . What is this?!' gargled poor Kirill.

'Oh, don't worry, darling,' cooed Heidi, tightening her grip. 'If you're a good little boy and keep still, this won't hurt at all.' And with her other hand, she grabbed his neck and wrenched off his chain!

'Aaargh!' cried Kirill.

RAARRGH! RAARRGH! chipped in Glitterpuff.

Kirill sank to the floor.

'That's . . . that's mine,' he gasped. 'My father gave it to me!'

'Ooooh yes, darling,' purred Heidi. 'I know all about your father.'

When she held up the chain, I felt as though my world had been flipped upside down. Dangling from the end was the last shape I was expecting: a gleaming miniature spatula. Before I could ask where Kirill's father got it or who he was, Heidi interrupted.

'Now, boys. Will you be so good as to press the button for the basement, please? Basements are *such* nice private places with no one around, aren't they, Gwitterpuffles?' She plunged the necklace into her coat. I guess I didn't have much choice. I raised my hand to the buttons and caught sight of my cufflinks. If you remember, these were the fish-shaped ones Camillo had given me. Filled with fishy superglue. I twisted the tail. A plan was sparking in my brain. There was every chance it could fail. But then again . . .

'Erm, I can't seem to work it, miss,' I mumbled. 'Sorry.'

'Pathetic! The children of today! It's a thrashing that you want, you little brat!'

The fur coat seemed to bristle with rage as she barged past me. I twiddled the fish tail again,

this time downwards.
I watched the tangerine
fingers press the button. Heidi was
one of those impatient types
who press a lift button a
million times, as if this
will make it move faster.

The doors opened. I grabbed Kirill's arm.

'Jump!'

There was a yowl, a bark and a *RIPPPP* as we
vaulted onto the basement floor. Glitterpuff had a
strip of trench coat in his jaws. Heidi Hyde High's
Botox-ed face finally showed some emotion.

'GET BACK HERE!!' she screeched. 'You
vermin! You fiends! You wretched little thugs!'

It had worked. Her finger was stuck to the
button, right on the blob of Camillo's superglue.
And Glitterpuff had stepped into the glue smeared
over the entrance. The combined effect of this was

that (a) every time HHH tried to yank her finger off the button it jerked back and pressed it again, and (b) this meant that the doors were forever opening and closing, clonking Glitterpuff. Heidi was dumb enough to press another button. Also glue-smeared. The doors finally shut and the lift shot off.

'Kirill,' I panted, '*where* did your family get that necklace?'

He dusted off his waistcoat.

'Yes, I will tell you. But first please, I need a *pishka*.'

Chapter 7

pishka was basically a Russian doughnut, but better, said Kirill. Snow was falling heavily now, splodging over the pavements. I thought bitterly of the warm fur coat that Swirly Ben had given me, left in the Hermitage cloakrooms. We passed two gold lions with lamps in their tails and crossed a bridge to an old cream-coloured building, lined with archways. Kirill darted through these and into a café. He bought a paper bag of *pishki*, all hot and squidgy. We watched the snow dollop outside in marzipan clumps. He told me about his necklace.

His father got it from his grandfather, who got it from his great-grandfather, who got it from his *great*-great-grandfather. Where he got it, no one knew. Kirill didn't think it was valuable. It wasn't actual gold. It was even a bit grubby. And what was so special about a mini spatula? Well, I could tell him lots of things that were special about mini spatulas. But just because his necklace had a spatula, did that mean it had anything to do with the G.S.L.?

'Kirill,' I said, 'can you tell me a bit more about your father? And what took him to Moscow?'

Kirill swallowed a chunk of *pishka*.

'Well . . . he was playing piano in a concert. But I remember . . . he was interested in this family story we have, about these egg cups, and I knew that recently he has been reading about them in the newspaper, and saw that they had been found. He was asking people who might know things about them.'

He crumpled up the paper bag and lobbed it bin-wards. It missed.

'He said there was a woman who was a famous expert in Brillerge eggs. From England, but she came to Moscow. He wanted to meet her there, to find out what happened to our . . . how do you say? Hair room?'

'Heirloom?' I suggested.

'Heirloom, yes. Well, he is one day late, and I still do not know what happened.'

'What was this woman's name?' I was fearing the worst.

'*Oγ* . . .' He drummed his sugary fingers on the table-top. 'I don't remember. But it began with H.'

'Were there lots of Hs?'

'Yes! Yes it was –'

'Kirill. I swear on my parents' pizzeria that the woman who stole your necklace in the lift is the same woman your dad was going to meet. I hate to break this to you, but she's a fully qualified psychopath.'

'Colin! How do you know all this? Can we please now go to the police?'

'Listen. I've got to tell you something. I'm not really an exchange student. And I'm not really a pizza delivery boy. I'm a de–'

BEEP-BEEP-BEEP-BEEP-BEEP-BEEP!

It was a video call from Princess.

'Yes?'

'What did I say about answering a call with the word "yes"?'

'Hi, Princess . . . what's up?'

'What's up is that Swirly Ben was spotted in a swanky restaurant on Nevsky Prospekt. As if he's about to meet someone. Hopefully not the pigtailed Grim Reaper. But I'd get over there ASAP just to be sure.'

'What's it called?'

'Beliseev's. The twins will be on hand. Over and out.'

Kirill raised an eyebrow.

'Girlfriend?'

'Hell, no.'

What Princess Skewer hadn't bothered to tell me was that Nevsky Prospekt was the longest street in St Petersburg. Pillowy banks of snow had submerged the benches and bins. Icicles erupted from broken drainpipes. Our breath hung against the ink-blue sky in crackly clouds. Trust me to lose a coat *designed* for this kind of weather. Finally, a tall edifice soared above us. The letters **B-E-L-I-S-E-E-V** spiked over its doors. Big bronze goddesses flanked the windows. Through the glowing patchwork of coloured panes I could see the hobbled outline of Swirly Ben, with his red beret and cascading beard. We crept in. He was seated on a circular couch at a tiny table, with a menu and some papers. The couch

was beneath a palm tree, which was squat like a
giant pineapple and hung with chandeliers. A grand
piano stood in the corner. There were some tanks of
live lobsters too. Poor chumps. Kirill got distracted
by a tower of macarons; I went to the back and
approached a skittering waiter.

'Ahem . . .'

'*Da?*' A snootyish boy looked down at me.

It wasn't the right place, but it was the right
time. I whipped off my shoe and sock, hoping the
whiff was the nearby gorgonzola. The
snootster peered at my
toe and saw my G.S.L.
tattoo.

'Ahhh . . .' His whole manner changed. '*Pre-
khoditye, pazhulasta . . .*'

He led me into the kitchens.

'Cooo-eeeeeee, darling!! Is Gwitterpuffles
hungry?'

I froze. My bladder seemed to implode. I spun around to face the music. It was Yelena and Yaconda. I felt like chucking a nearby jelly at them.

'I thought we'd guard the back, Anchovy,' said Yelena – still in Heidi's voice, which I resented.

'No, Lena, it was *my* idea to guard the back,' said Yaconda, now trying out Pudders' scratchy drawl. 'You said we would guard the front and *Anchovy* would guard the back!'

'Both great ideas either way,' I cut in. 'But can one of you tell me what is happening?'

Yaconda threw me a uniform.

'Wear this and take out the posh pizza.'

Yelena wheeled over a trolley with a silver platter.

'Urgh!' I said. 'Is that a *caviar* pizza?'

'Whatever floats your boat,' said Yelena.

'As I was saying,' said Yaconda, in something approaching a normal voice, 'take this out and guard Swirly Ben.'

'From who? Heidi and the Werewolf?'

I flung on the uniform. Somewhere in my secret office there's a manual titled *Essential Super-Speedy Dressing*.

'We'll help if there's trouble. Just watch him. He's acting very weirdly.'

'Well, yeah, he just ordered a caviar pizza,' I said, and took out the platter.

A figure was advancing to Swirly Ben's table. She was a nervous-looking woman in a powder-blue suit and a pearl-stud bow tie. She had short silvery curls and a face as pale and soft as a marshmallow.

'Mr Ben? Mr Swirly? How do you prefer?' She inclined her head. 'Professor Peshkova at your service.'

With his trembling, purplish hand, Swirly Ben gestured to the seat opposite. He caught sight of me with the caviar pizza.

I placed it on the little table and loitered around the palm tree.

'I understand, Mr Ben . . . er, Mr Swirly . . . er, however you prefer . . .' bumbled Professor Peshkova, 'that you have some important information for my colleagues and me at the museum?'

Who is Professor Peshkova? I typed to Princess.

Director of the Brillerge Museum. It was in the brief.

'Regarding the Brillerge egg cups?' the professor tried again.

Swirly Ben sat motionless. Then the beard spoke:

'All the lockets,

Lock it above.

All will unbox it,

Shocking doves.'

What was it with this guy and riddles?

'Well!' cried Professor Peshkova. 'What a

charming little poem. But er . . . what about the Brillerge egg cups, Mr Ben . . . er . . . Mr Swirly . . . however you –'

She stopped short. Swirly Ben had reached into his coat pocket and pulled out something very small and very fine. It was a necklace. A necklace with a mini spatula on the end. Kirill was agog. I turned around and motioned for him to stay where he was.

'Ah, Mr Ben, Mr Swirly,' said the professor, 'I think we are beginning to see eye to eye.'

And now she pulled something from her jacket. Also a necklace. Also with a mini spatula. I was so stunned that I didn't clock who had just entered the restaurant.

Hide your face, beeped Princess on my watch.

'Yooohooo, darlingsssss!'

I suppose it *could* have been the twins. But I wasn't going to check. The snooty waiter gave me a sly G.S.L. glance and passed by with a trolley. I grabbed one of his platters with the fancy lids and held it up to my face. In the reflection I caught sight of the white fur coat, and the colossal dog-wolf trailing behind.

'Oh darlings, I hope you don't mind me joining your little picnic, *do* you? Three is *such* a lovely number, isn't it?'

'Oh, um . . . have we *met*?' quavered the professor.

'Oh dear, don't you know who I am?' cried Heidi, her voice skidding into manic laughter. 'Perhaps *this* will interest you.'

From her avalanche of fur, she pulled out the third spatula necklace. Poor Kirill.

'A darling little darling, isn't it, darling?' she purred, and turned the carved spatula over in the glow of the chandeliers. 'And now, here's what you two little turtle doves are going to do for me: you're going to give me those teeny tiny necklaces.' She craned her vulture neck over the papers on the table. 'Ah . . . yes, then we're all going to take a nice jolly train to Moscow, to those dear little Brillerges I'm so fond of. Aren't we?' She pulled out a tin – about the shape and size of a hockey puck – and placed it on the table. 'And in exchange, darlings, I will give you this ever so special little gift.'

I could just about read the label: 'Heidi Hyde High's High-class Caviar (London)'.

Princess beeped:

Round about now might be a good time to, you know, do something.

'Stop!' I said feebly, lowering the platter.

'You!!!' screeched Heidi Hyde High.

But I was too late.

Professor Peshkova had opened the tin of caviar.

'Ooooh!'

Black smoke started to bubble out. Within seconds, diners and waiters alike were slumping to the floor. Everything from then on was a blur. Dimly, I saw Heidi Hyde High hold a handkerchief to her face, lean over the wilting professor and snatch her necklace. Choking on the fumes, I remembered what Camillo, inventor extraordinaire, had said about my G.S.L.-issue Russian hat.

It contains an oxygen mask when you pull this . . .

I yanked down the front flap, which clipped over my face, and inhaled deeply from some cleverly concealed oxygen supply. The snooty waiter was trying to drag Professor Peshkova to safety. Swirly Ben was fumbling at his beard while scrambling away. The twins rushed out to grab him before Glitterpuff did. Heidi went for me. I did the only thing I could do in that nano-second. I flung the platter at her. Its fancy lid – it's called a cloche, I remember now – frisbeed off. The contents couldn't have been better chosen: one very tetchy lobster. It clung like a magnet, mangling her pigtails.

'AAAAAAAAAARGGGHHHHHHH!!!!!!!!!!!'
she screamed, collapsing in a ball. Swirly Ben
was gone. I swept up his papers and charged to
the kitchen. Kirill was by a fridge, bamboozled.
The twins had chucked a vat of pea soup over
Glitterpuff. He skidded around like Bambi on ice,
dropping something fluffy from his slavering jaws. I
swooped in and grabbed it.

'Where did Swirly Ben go?'

'I thought you had him, Yack?'

'I thought *you* had him, Lena?'

'Move! Move!' I shouted, hurtling out of the
back door. But the lane was empty.

All I could hear was the gentle slosh of the
canal as snow gathered on the cobbles. How could
someone so decrepit be so slippery? In the lamplight
I looked again at the fluffy rag in my hands. Swirly
Ben certainly was old-school. It was a false beard.

Chapter 8

'Pssssst!'

An invisible hisser lingered in the shadows. A second *psst* sounded. Then a third, from below the railings. I peered down at the canal. One foot on a barge, the other on the steps, stood a girl in a fur-lined jacket – and a fur-lined eye patch.

'Welcome to Russia, Mr Anchovy.'

I remembered her: the G.S.L. air steward with the laxative fish.

'Please – it is cold,' she said. 'Tell your friends to come aboard.'

The sight of another river barge made me
shudder, as I remembered my fiery ride in
Rufflington. But when you're two eyebrows short
of a face, you've not got much else to lose. Yelena,
Yaconda and Kirill came over and we hopped
down onto the boat and into a wood-panelled cabin
with purple cushions, a narrow table, a battered tea
urn and a chirpy-looking heater, glowing orange.
Yelena and Yaconda squabbled over the seat next

to it. We nestled close and warmed up our cherry Bakewell faces.

'Welcome, dear friends,' said the laxative fishmonger. 'My name is Anna Z. Afanasyeva, Russian G.S.L. But everyone calls me Anchka.'

'Anchka?' I said. 'That's like my name.'

'Yes, a little,' said Anchka.

'Anchka is not like the name Colin at all, Colin,' said Kirill.

'You should call him Anchovy!' blared Yelena, in a corny superhero voice.

'Anchovy is his name,' whispered Yaconda, in a wildlife documentary voice.

'*Anchovy?*' Kirill stopped tapping and did a double take.

'Mark Anchovy,' I said. 'It's a sort of nickname.'

Anchka held out a tin box. 'Would anybody like a pipe?'

A pipe? Even G-pops didn't smoke a pipe.

'I think she means,' said Kirill, opening the tin, 'a sweet pipe, or as we call them in Russia, a *troobuchka*, which means "little pipe".' He took a tube-shaped wafer and bit into it, lapping up the caramel goo inside. '*Spaseeba*.' We copied him.

'There is *chai* also,' said Anchka, pointing at the tea urn. 'I will explain more at our destination.'

She went to the front of the boat and took the wheel. We slid off into the night, the ice floes crackling. I was glad to be here, with tea and a *troobuchka*, and no maniac in sight.

'Stop hogging the heater, Yack!' bawled Yelena.

'You were hogging it to begin with!' snapped Yaconda.

'Why don't you just share?' I muttered, trying to enjoy my pipe in peace.

'Yes,' said Kirill, drumming on the tin, 'Colin has a good idea. Sharing is better.'

I watched the occasional tour boat floating by.

The canal spewed us out onto the main river, which was veiled in fog. I could make out the mansions on the embankment, twinkling like a toytown. Peeking above was the Church of the Spilled Blood and the minty stretch of the Hermitage. I dug out the papers from Swirly Ben's table.

'I didn't know you had friends in Russia, Colin,' said Kirill. 'And I didn't know that people call you Anchovy!'

'There's a lot you don't know, Kirill.' I sank into the purple plush and listened to the hum of the engine. I thought about Swirly Ben. About where he was going and what he wanted. Between the tenth and eleventh *troobuchka*, the barge pulled in. We slung on our coats and followed Anchka into the snow. She stopped at a derelict building that had a tower like a lighthouse. Its whole side was painted with a flaking mural. It showed someone in a spacesuit, riding a chocolate bar through space, flashing a toothy grin. We shunted up a fire escape until Anchka reached this toothy grin. Then she banged on one of the teeth, chanting the G.S.L. motto:

'*Aureum in spatha est, vivat in spatha.*'

We waited. I took it that this tooth was a door.

'Did you know that the first woman in space was a Russian?' said Anchka. 'Also the first man. Also the first dog.'

I wondered what other pets had been blasted into orbit. A hamster, maybe? That would be a tricky spacesuit to manufacture. Anchka banged on the tooth-door again. It was opened by a girl with red dungarees and a kindly smile. We filed in.

'This place was a chocolate factory,' said Anchka, 'but was abandoned a long time ago.'

'What, no more chocolate?' moaned Yelena.

'You just had about twenty *troobuchki*,' said Yaconda.

'Twelve, Yack!'

We clambered across a network of iron walkways over dusty, crater-like cauldrons that had once swirled with pools of Russian chocolate. A canopy of strange lamps hung over the warehouse, like a bric-a-brac solar system. There were lamp-post lights, train lights, rusty chandeliers, pinkish laboratory lights – even the odd half-broken floodlight from a stadium.

'One of your colleagues is here already,' said Anchka.

An old lift took us two floors down. The doors opened to reveal a nose-picking Camillo in a sheepskin jacket. He pretended to wipe his snot on the twins, and got a dead arm from both of them.

'*Ciao*, Anchovy! Ah, I should say "*Preevyet*, Anchovy" since we are in Russia now. How did you find the Hoverbog?'

105

'I'd rather not go into it, Cam,' I said. 'This is Kirill, by the way.'

Camillo shook Kirill's hand warmly (which was very unhygienic of him), then nodded at the fluffy rag poking from my pocket.

'What's that?'

I handed it over.

'A false beard.'

Camillo smiled.

'No, Anchovy. It is a gas mask.'

He pulled back the straggles of beard, revealing some old-fashioned breathing apparatus. I thought back to Beliseev's, when I'd seen Swirly Ben fumbling at his beard. He had been putting on his gas mask!

'Where would he have got a thing like this?'

'I think we are about to find out, Anchovy.'

We took off our coats and boots, were given slippers by the girl in the red dungarees, and

entered a long, brick-vaulted room. The far
wall was stacked with display cases. To one side,
Russian delegates in headphones watched a bank
of television monitors, with live feeds from G.S.L.
stations. I had a similar, smaller set-up in my secret
office beneath Caesar Pizza. (Which Alicia was
probably ransacking at this very moment.) There
was also a 3D map of Russia with lightbulbs
flashing blue and red.

Anchka gathered us in a semi-circle.

'I believe we are here, dear friends, colleagues,'
she said, 'because we are all searching for the same
old man.'

'Swirly Ben!' I exclaimed.

Anchka frowned.

'Here we call him by his original Russian name,
Ulitka Venya.'

The room seemed to wobble, the red and blue
map lights clustering like flies.

'Swirly Ben is *Russian*?'

There was a collective gasp from the Russian delegates. Anchka narrowed her eye at me.

'Do you not know who is Ulitka – *oy* – who is Swirly Ben?'

It was like being in a history lesson, when Hogstein makes you feel like an absolute turkey for not knowing about some medieval randomer.

'Er, no . . . sorry.'

'The man you call Swirly Ben,' she continued, sighing deeply, 'is a hero of the Russian G.S.L.'

Chapter 9

'**S**wirly Ben?' I stammered. 'G.S.L.?'

That explained his vanishing acts. His novelty gas mask. His overly elaborate methods.

'It is interesting that in British G.S.L. history exams,' sighed Anchka, 'you are taught some things but not other things. Come this way, please, friends.' She indicated the wall of display cases. Inside these were yellowing papers, photographs and ornaments.

'Here he is.' She pointed to an ID card. I couldn't read the text, but I could see it was dated

1916. The G.S.L. logo was stamped in blue ink
and it had a passport-sized photograph of a wide-
eyed boy in a beret. Have you ever put tinfoil in a
microwave? Don't. Really, really don't. It's just that
my brain was doing what the tinfoil does. Buzzing.
Fizzing. Exploding. I had seen this wide-eyed boy
in a beret before . . .

'Ulitka Venya – let's call him Swirly Ben so
you don't get confused,' said Anchka, 'belonged
to a small group of detectives, working in
restaurants and cafés, and was famous in Russian
G.S.L. circles. He was apprentice to a pastry
chef.'

'Was this a million years ago?' said Yaconda.

'It was a hundred years ago, Yack,' said Yelena.

Kirill was looking curious. Camillo had pressed
his runny nose against the glass.

Anchka pulled out a drawer of knick-knacks. I
spotted a line of pin badges, with the faces of young

Swirly Ben, and others who also seemed familiar.

'When we were training for the G.S.L., we studied the cases of Swirly Ben,' continued Anchka. 'We got these special badges for passing our exams. It's crazy – he was only five years old when he joined.'

'That *is* crazy,' I agreed. Five years old?

Sure enough, Swirly Ben's face was everywhere in this mini museum: on calendars, diaries, bookmarks, soap bars, pencil cases, lunch boxes, chocolate wrappers and strange wooden toys with the paint peeling off.

'Why don't we get this kind of merch?' said Yelena.

'And what made Swirly Ben so famous?' said Yaconda.

'Probably you already know about his very first case, since you are working on it,' said Anchka.

'The Brillerge egg cups,' I said.

'Correct. Which brings me' – she faced Kirill – 'to you.'

'The Brillerge egg cups . . .' Kirill said slowly. '. . . but they are missing.'

'Yes, Kirill. You see' – she scowled at the slime Camillo had left on the glass – 'your ancestors paid the G.S.L. to find the Brillerge egg cups, after a gang of jewellery thieves had stolen them in 1916. Swirly Ben and his colleagues found them in 1917. But they were never able to give them back.'

'Because of the Revolution, *kanyeshna*,' said Kirill.

'Correct.'

Damn, I knew that one.

'Unfortunately,' said Anchka, 'when the Revolution came, everything connected with the G.S.L. was banished and replaced with a new organisation.'

'What were they called?' asked Camillo.

'The Associated Red Spoons,' said Anchka, without blinking.

'So Swirly Ben had to leave?' said Yelena.

'Everyone in the G.S.L. had to leave,' said Yaconda. 'Duh.'

'So,' I added, trying to get my egg cups straight. 'The G.S.L. fled, they left the egg cups here, and Swirly Ben – in his potty, cryptic way – wants us to help him close the case.'

'That's it,' said Anchka.

But one last thing was bugging me.

'Why is everyone tearing lumps out of each other for these spatula necklaces?' I asked.

Kirill tugged his collar, at the gap where his necklace once hung.

Anchka's eye widened.

'We have heard about these necklaces, Anchovy. But we know very little about them. Many important records and documents were destroyed in 1917.'

'I think we should call Princess,' said Camillo.

'Okaaaay.' I sighed, bracing myself.

Anchka led us to the wall of monitors and addressed the girl in the red dungarees.

'*Tamara, mozhesh pozvonit v London, pozhaluysta . . .*'

She got dialling. Princess Skewer's face popped onto the monitor.

'*Dobriy vecher*, Anchka,' she said. 'Anchovy, what's up?'

'A lot's up.'

I brought her up to speed with our colourful day of sightseeing in St Petersburg. She was silent for a while. I wasn't sure if (a) the signal was bad and the picture on the screen was frozen or (b) she was just brooding, loading up her venom. Sadly, the answer was (b).

'Let me get this straight, Anchovy. You've lost

Swirly Ben. You also lost the coat he gave you, which could've been crucial evidence. And worst of all, you've let three vital G.S.L. spatula necklaces out of your sight, two of them to that demented caviar-chomper, Heidi Hyde High!' She really drew out the 'Highhhh!!', blasting it out like a brass band.

'*Three* spatula necklaces,' Anchka muttered, head in hands.

'You're right about the second part, Princess,' I said. 'But I know where Swirly Ben is.'

I brought out the papers he had left in the restaurant. They included a train timetable, with a circle drawn around the 22:05 to Moscow.

'He's catching the sleeper tonight?' said Yelena.

'That's thirty minutes from now!' added Yaconda, in a scared chipmunk voice.

'Okay, okay,' said Princess, massaging her temples. 'Camillo: hack into the station cameras and keep an eye out for Swirly Ben. Twins: get out there and locate Heidi Hyde High. It's possible she'll go after Swirly Ben and board that train. Anchka: can you prep your Moscow delegates, please? Anchovy: head to the station and radio the others. You're going to steal back those spatulas and save Swirly Ben.'

She made it sound like I was just nipping out to buy a pint of milk.

'And Kirill: hang in there. We'll get back your egg cups.'

'Can I go with Colin? I mean, Anchovy?' said Kirill.

'I think he needs all the help he can get,' said Princess. 'Over and out.'

'Good luck, friends,' said Anchka and passed us her light-blue calling cards. 'We are very glad to be working with you on this.'

We headed out of the old factory, past the

chocolate cauldrons, through the spaceman's
tooth-door, and parted by the canal. The fog had
thickened, cobwebbed over the spires and railings.
I yanked down the flaps of my hat and beat my
gloved hands together to keep warm.

Kirill hailed a rickety old tram and we ploughed
through the snow. Crowds were pouring into the
train station past chunky policemen in camouflage.
On the ceiling was a painting of people in overalls,
waving red flags over a sunset sky. They were all
staring at the same bald guy with the goatee –
the one whose statue I saw before I landed. We
watched all the people – saying hello, saying
goodbye, with their cases, their big chequered bags,
their pushchairs, their cat baskets, their guitar cases,
their gymnastics hoops, their vats of red berries.
Hogstein's worksheets flickered in my memory.
Here were travellers from as far away as Yakutsk,
Ulan-Ude, Kamchatka, Cheboksary, Sakhalin.

They would have been on the trains for over twenty hours, covering a country one-sixth of the earth's land mass. In comparison, Rufflington-on-Sea was just a speck of dust. Kirill, curse him, chose this moment to go and pee. We had six minutes until the train. The pizza watch beeped. It was Princess.

Board the 22:05.

How? I replied, after opening my wallet and imagining a cartoon moth flying out of it.

Improvise. You're G.S.L.

Lost in thought, I saw the advancing figure too late to react. It lurched above the crowd, wearing a beret. Actually, it wasn't *quite* a beret, more of a Scottish bonnet or something. But why am I going on about the hat? It was the face beneath it that was the problem.

'Well, well, well, Kingsley! One might call this fate, eh?'

As close as I'd been to catching pneumonia outside, I now shot to the opposite end of the thermostat. My beetroot face was burning. My armpits reverted back to Lake Titicacas.

'Oh . . . uh . . . er . . . hello, Mr Hogstein.'

Chapter 10

He went bananas. I mean, if he ever got tired of being a teacher/dictator, he could easily get a job as a station announcer. I say this because he was actually louder than the poor guy trying to announce the trains over a proper loudspeaker. Everyone was staring at us as he went into meltdown.

'THIS IS OUTRAGEOUS, BOY! OUTRAGEOUS, DO YOU HEAR ME?!'

(Funny question, given that there were probably people in Vladivostok who could hear him.)

'HOW DARE YOU RUN AWAY FROM
YOUR HOST FAMILY?! HOW DARE YOU?!
DO YOU KNOW HOW MANY PEOPLE
HAVE BEEN PUT OUT JUST SO YOU
CAN . . .'

My eardrum may have burst, or I may have been distracted by the fact that I needed to board a train and find a slippery egg-smuggler, but I tuned out.

Board the 22:05.

It was 22:00 now! I scanned the board.
Platform 8.

'ARE YOU EVEN LISTENING TO ME,
YOUNG MAN? WHAT IS THE MATTER
WITH YOU?!!'

Encouragingly, there were no ticket barriers. Less encouragingly, a man with a toilet-brush attached to his face was also heading for Platform 8. Unkle Pudders, in his potato-sack coat. It's amazing what fear does to your calf muscles. I'd never been that quick on sports day. But right now I could've outpaced a cheetah. Hogstein's shock gave me a head start but, to be fair to the old waffler, he had a decent turn of pace.

'GET BACK HERE, KINGSLEY! GET BACK!'

Unkle Pudders sprang – if a man that bulky *can* spring – to life.

'You!!' he croaked, before joining the chase.

Platform 8 was rammed. There was only so much ducking and dodging I could do through the scrum of suitcases and passengers. Hogstein was gaining on me. Pudders, a few rows back, was hot on our heels. And at the end of the platform, more chilling than a Siberian wind, was Heidi Hyde High and her hellhound. She saw me straight away. I couldn't go forward. I couldn't go back. I couldn't go sideways. That would mean (a) barging past some tourists with giant

rucksacks, (b) vaulting a train guard in a scary
Thunderbirds uniform, and (c) boarding the train
without a ticket. Then I compared this with the
alternative. The rucksacks-on-legs were arguing
about their e-tickets. Thunderbird Lady had to
decide between chasing me or letting on these
other ticket-dodgers. I charged on and wriggled
up the carriage. Thunderbird Lady squawked. In
the narrow corridor, compartment doors were
sliding open and shut. Passengers squished past in
flip-flops, queuing for a toilet, a tea urn, a mini-
kiosk. There was shouting from the platforms. It
might have been Hogstein. It might have been
Pudders. Up ahead there was a Heidi-ish shriek.
I edged past the compartments, drawing up my
collar. Everyone was on bunkbeds in their nighties
and vests, playing on their phones, drinking
funky milk. It was a sleeper train. The journey to
Moscow would take – I recalled the Departures

board – eleven hours! I was on this death wagon for eleven hours! The shouting from outside grew louder. I had a dim impression of Hogstein arguing with the guards. *CRASH* went the door between the carriages, slamming in frustration. I was flung against the wall. We were moving! St Petersburg was sliding away behind me. But what about Kirill?

'Come on, lad! We know you're in here!'

It was the gravelly rasp of Pudders. Heaving open the doors, I bolted to the next carriage. And the next one. The train thundered on, the Pud-sack booming after me.

'The game is up, son! You got nowhere to run!'

Another voice joined him, but from the opposite direction.

'Where are you? Where are you, you disgusting snot-stain? Come on, Glitterpuff! Mummy's very, very angry with that *silly* little boy! Where are you?'

'Come on, sonny!' growled Pudders from along the passage. 'The game is up!'

It was a fair point. The game did seem up. I was supposed to sneak onto this train and stealthily pinch a golden spatula necklace. But that purple-faced Hog-muppet had ruined everything. Footsteps drew nearer. In desperation, I flung open a compartment. It was full of nighties and eye masks and toes poking from blankets, cursing at me. I wasn't all that keen on asking if I could hide under one of their duvets.

'Come on, sonny!' came the growl.

'Come out, you foul bandit!' came the shriek.

I reached the last compartment. Now there were just toilets. And kiosks. And a sleeping cabin for the guards. And a linen cupboard. I dived in. Now, finally, I appreciated my training in G.S.L. contortion. I found a shelf, bent myself into a Z-shape, and draped myself in as many packs of towels, sheets and blankets as I could find. A screech-off was taking place in the corridor.

'Where is he, Pudders?'

'I thought you had him, Miss Heidi.'

'Do I *look* like I have him, you cloth-headed fuzz-mumbler?'

'Er, no, miss.'

'Check the toilets.'

A door crashed open.

'Oops – sorry, sir.'

On boomed the train. Or perhaps it was my heart.

'Here's what you're going to do, Pudders. You're going to walk down the length of this train and open every compartment in every carriage. And when you do that, Puddy dear, you are going to turf out every passenger, one by one, until you find this disgusting little excrescence!'

'Yes, miss.'

There was a pause as she reloaded. 'Unless . . .'
She rattled the linen cupboard. 'Open this.'

Light flooded in.

'Hmmm,' purred Heidi Hyde High. I lay there,
towelled up to the max, holding my breath.

'I do, er, have *some* good news, Miss Heidi,' the
fuzz-mumbler said.

'Oh? *Do* you now, darling? And what is that?
Have you finally decided to shave off that revolting
hair-turd?' She slammed the door, apparently
satisfied.

'Heh-heh, er no, Miss Heidi.'

My heart skipped a beat as I strained to hear.

'I've caught Swirly Ben.'

Chapter 11

He was probably getting de-spatulaed at this very moment. Still, I reflected between fitful naps, he was doing better than I was. Only my second assignment and I had royally fluffed up.

If I'd been a seasoned contortionist, with more than just a Grade One certificate, I might have held that Z-shape for eleven hours and stayed hidden. But I couldn't. Around five in the morning the door was wrenched open. It was the train guard, AKA Thunderbird Lady.

Although I'd only been in Russia for a few

days, I was starting to understand the language. Particularly if it was the language of a telling-off. I'd love to have seen this lady and Hogstein in a shouting match. She was properly going for it. Something about a ticket (like the French, *beelyet*) and '*where? where? where?*' seemed to be the gist. My shrugging and gibbering only made her angrier. She stepped in, grabbed my collar and flung me out like a pile of dirty sheets. Perhaps this made me flip, or perhaps it was instinct, but I spotted a ruse. Thunderbird Lady was now standing in the cupboard. I was in the corridor. I booted the door shut and yanked the handle upwards, praying to the pizza gods that was how it locked. The pizza gods heard me. Thunderbird Lady was stuck. It was a bit harsh, I know. But it was either that or let all hell break loose on a defenceless 108-year-old who could only speak in riddles.

I tried to remember my G.S.L. training. *If you're*

looking for a safe zone, look for the kitchen. I went
through the carriages. The compartments were
a moonlit forest of feet. Ghostly birches flashed
outside, zebra-striped. I passed a glowing furnace,
then stepped over a juddering join in the carriages,
then sidled past some groggy men in vests who
were shaving, then crept along a deserted buffet
car. Finally, I found a kiosk laden with snacks, a
till, a microwave, a fridge, dozens of drawers, tea,
coffee and a trolley of foil-covered trays. On this
was a bottle of champagne, two glasses and a pot of
something that looked like rabbit poo. Something
that only a demented diva like Heidi Hyde High
would request for breakfast. Caviar. It was labelled
'2A'.

There was no G.S.L. worker in sight, so I'd have
to fly solo. I scanned the labels on the drawers, not
even sure what I was looking for. Unsurprisingly,
I hadn't mastered the Cyrillic alphabet. Reaching

for Camillo's mini phrase book didn't really help. I doubt any of the drawers said 'Where is the nearest pharmacy, please?' or 'Sorry, but I'm allergic to mayonnaise'. But the bottom right drawer was different. It had a number dial, like those found on safes. Although I didn't have my magnifying glass (I know, rookie), I could just make out the shape above the dial.

What combination would open-sesame it? Simple. 1-8-6-7. The year the league was founded. The drawer contained an on-board catering crew's uniform; binoculars; some edible notebooks and pencils; a harpoon fountain pen; a hairnet gas mask; a flashlight with a G.S.L. hologram-generator; and a medical kit marked 'sedatives'. Most of these items I puzzled over. But the last one gave me a brainwave.

I remembered that on the flight Anchka had fed Glitterpuff a sedative doggy chew. If I put sedatives in Heidi's caviar and sent her to sleep, *maybe* I could get those mini-spatula necklaces back – and hopefully rescue poor old Swirly Ben.

Smuggling a couple of tablets into the pot of ~~rabbit poo~~ caviar was easy enough. The champagne, not so much. I couldn't exactly uncork it then reseal it. I took a chance and crumbled the tablets into a fine dust in the glasses. I was about to slip into the train caterer's uniform when a *CRASH-BANG-WALLOP* echoed from the corridor. Followed by some cursing. Thunderbird Lady was on the loose. In the heat of the moment I chose the weirdest place possible to hide. I opened the food trolley, removed the middle shelf and the trays of mashed potato. Proving I was ready for Grade Two contortion after all, I shoved myself inside: knees first, chin tucked into my navel, every bone going clackety-clack, using my rolled-up trench coat as a pillow. While I still had the power of my limbs, I whipped out the purée gun and fired against the inner wall. It lasered me a nice little peephole. I slid the door back just as Thunderbird Lady thundered into view. Even her ankles looked angry. I heard the sort of bellowing you might mistake for a World War Two air-raid siren. Added to this, the trolley started moving. And I realised now that my hiding place was accidentally perfect. Thunderbird Lady was delivering the breakfasts. And in doing so, she was delivering me. I just hoped no one else had ordered caviar. Or extra mashed potato. On she wheeled, rapping on doors, bellowing her breakfast bugle. Through the peephole, I watched compartment doors slide open and blinds roll up. Squashed in that sweat-box, I decided that if we played Twister at Christmas, I'd win with almost embarrassing ease. We rolled on.

I saw the first-class compartments. Thunderbird Lady opened the first door. Number 2A. My heart thudded. There were just two beds in these compartments – bigger, plusher, covered in red tassels and extra pillows. One had a wolf in it. The other a Heidi Hyde High. Swirly Ben was nowhere to be seen.

'*Dobriy ootra!*' shouted Thunderbird Lady. She left the trolley in the corridor and bustled in with breakfast. The bed buddies stirred. Heidi wore a face pack and hairnet. More alarmingly, two gold chains hung from her neck, under her PJs.

'What-what-what . . . what is the *meaning* of this?'

'Please, madam, we arrive in Moscow in forty minutes. Your breakfast, please.'

'Ooooooh,' cooed Heidi. 'Caviar and champers! Gwitterpuffle's favourite treat! But mummy wummy *must* feed it to him, mustn't she?'

She necked the champagne and dug into the caviar.

'Cooooeeee, come here, Gwitterpuffles, brekkie wekkie time . . .'

Four clawed paws left the bed. I didn't bother watching the feeding routine. What I could hear was nauseating enough. The chomping, the panting, the baby talk. Thunderbird Lady poured more champagne. The sedative trick was predictable but effective. Sometimes it's good to keep it simple. Pretty soon the caviar-chompers were snoring. When Thunderbird Lady transferred her attention to another compartment, I slipped open the trolley door, gasping like a drowning man, and rolled into the first-class wolf pit.

I shuddered at the snoring Heidi. The gold chains glimmered against her tangerine collarbone. On the floor, Glitterpuff twitched with dreams of chewing trousers. My hands were shaking. I closed a delicate finger and thumb around the chains, as if I was clasping a butterfly. I lifted up the necklaces, hoping I wouldn't wake Heidi, but the drugged champagne worked – for now. I pulled, and the spatulas emerged from her PJs. But when they slithered across her throat, she made a noise.

'No!' she grumbled. 'No! I was told the breakfast was *complimentary*, darling! I'm not paying that! I'm telling you . . . I'm telling you . . .'

She was sleep-talking.

'Do you know who I *am*?' she murmured to a poor dream-minion. 'Do you . . .' she whimpered and dozed off again.

Sweat was trickling into my eyes. I took a deep breath, lifted the necklaces up over her face pack and hairnet, and pocketed them. *Ker-ching*.

I typed to Princess: **Got the spatula necklaces. Looking for Swirly Ben.**

Roger.

(Who the heck was Roger?)

Open the window.

What, did she think Swirly Ben would be
strapped to the roof? I drew the curtains, hoisted
up the window and looked around. All I could see
was forest and snowclad meadows, electric blue in
the dawn. A vicious whirl of snow blasted around
the cabin. It didn't seem to bother the out-for-the-
count Heidi, or Glitterpuff.

No sign of SB, I typed.

Have you tried under the seat?

How was a 108-year-old man supposed to
survive in a foetal position under a bed/seat? Even
if he had done Grade *Eight* contortion, it was a
big ask. Still, leave no stone unturned. There was
a lever by Glitterpuff's vacated bed. I yanked it,
shoved, and the bed folded up. A rumpled figure
lay below.

Well?

I slammed the seat back down, hoping it would make the problem go away. I felt like I couldn't breathe, or think, or move, or do anything.

Have you got him?!!

I rang her.

'Anchovy, have you got Swirly Ben?'

'Princess . . .' I huffed. 'The man on the train . . .'

Breathe, Colin, breathe.

'The man under the seat . . .'

It was like a nightmare. Those unmistakable jowls. Those goldfish-bowl glasses. That purple flush.

'Yes? Yes? Spit it out, Anchovy!'

That big bald dome.

'The man they've captured . . .'

Huff huff

Those angry beaver teeth . . .

'The man they've captured is not . . .'

Come on, Colin.

'The man they've captured is *not* Swirly Ben.'

Silence. Only the kind of static you hear before thunder.

'Okaaaay,' said Princess with rising venom. 'THEN WHO THE FLUFF IS HE?!'

Somehow I got it out.

'My history teacher.'

Chapter 12

ntil this point, Heidi and Glitterpuff had been snoring like the dead. Even the snow whipping into the cabin hadn't woken them. But if there's one thing that can stir the dead, it's the wrath of an outraged Hogstein.

'Good lord!' he choked, revving up. 'KINGSLEY! OF ALL THE –'

Glitterpuff sleep-growled. Heidi whimpered. Before my brain could compute what my hand was doing, I had grabbed Hogstein by the jowls, opened his mouth, and shoved the champagne into the abyss.

'What the dickens –' he gargled. 'Oh, oh . . .'
He became drowsy in an instant.

'Such a velvety mousse . . . very refreshing . . .
but . . . what . . . what . . .'

A new chorus of snoring filled the
compartment.

'Move!' shouted Princess over the pizza watch.

Normally I wouldn't be able to lift a two-
ton history teacher. But fear can be a curious
superpower. I lugged him by the bingo wings. He
was stirring a bit now, the icy wind reviving him.

'What the . . . what . . . what . . .'

'To the window!' Princess heckled.

'Princess, I'm not going to lob my history
teacher out of a moving train.'

'I wouldn't say "lob", Anchovy. More
"accompany".'

'What?'

'You are also leaving through that window.'

'Hold on –'

'Well, well, well! I thought I smelt a nasty little rat! *You!*' Heidi Hyde High craned out of bed. Her PJs were terrifyingly sheer. She nudged the wolf with a fluffy bunny slipper.

'Wake up, Glitterpuff! Wake up!!'

'Now, Anchovy!'

'What . . . what . . .' mumbled Hogstein, before sinking back into slumber. I squidged him up onto the windowsill. Hunched over, his jowls flapping, he looked like a doddery retriever struggling to get into a car boot. I did actually feel quite sorry for him.

'Oh no, you don't!' snapped Heidi, and prodded the wolf again. Flicker-flicker, went the gas-flame eyes.

RARRGH RARRGH! RARRGH! RARRGH!

I looked out of the window. The forest gave way to a high ridge of snow. Smoke wafted from some wooden houses below.

RARRGH RARRGH! RARRGH! RARRGH!

Glitterpuff repeated, as if I hadn't got the memo
the first time. Hogstein swayed on the windowsill.
I stared down at the snowy precipice. Then at the
chasm of Glitterpuff's gullet.

'GET THEM, GLITTERPUFF!' screamed
Heidi. 'GET THEM FOR MUMMY!'

Spying the food tray, I was reminded of when
Alicia and I went sledging. Our parents didn't have
a sledge or toboggan. So what had we used? A
dinner tray. I sprayed it with fish-glue, slammed it
against Hogstein's barn door of a backside, jumped
on his back, and catapulted us into the winter
wonderland.

'Noooooooooo!!!' screeched Heidi Hyde High.
'He's got the spatulaaaaaaaaaas! Noooooooooo!!!'

WHUUMFFFFFF went the Hog-sledge as he
jetted onto the slope. By some miracle, he landed
tray-first. Gravity did the rest. Hogstein sagged

over as we plummeted. It was like trying to steer a space hopper. The wooden houses drew nearer. And still the Hog-sledge raced on, puffing up the powder, clearing a stream, barging through chicken wire, until *WHAM!* A fence brought us to a standstill. I rolled off his shoulders and looked back. The train had vanished on the bone-white horizon.

A few rooks squawked, mockingly.

Poor Hogstein. He hadn't had the smoothest arrival: mugged, drugged, and shoved from a train. Also, he now had a dinner tray superglued to his XXL chinos. He probably needed a St Bernard dog to give him a hug and a brandy or something. I could see how it had happened. Take a man like Unkle Pudders. A man who has mashed potatoes where the rest of us have brain cells. He had seen me at the station, talking in English to an old-ish guy in a beret-bonnet-thing. He'd probably been told that Swirly Ben was now beardless. And his potato-cells had put two and two together and made eight. It was the mother of all fluff-ups. You would think Heidi Hyde High would start advertising for a new henchman right away.

I pulled Hogstein through the gap between the houses, where I could see a few cars. A hobbled-over granny was feeding some ducks. I had a plan, but I needed a translator. I dialled Anchka.

Chapter 13

Here was my plan, all expenses covered by the G.S.L. Step one: Order a taxi. Step two: Order a suite at a swanky Moscow hotel. Step three: forge a doc from the train company saying they were extremely sorry for Mr Hogstein's troublesome journey and that by way of compensation they were putting him up in the grand old Metropole, or wherever it was, free of charge. Step four: find a pizza, preferably with anchovies. I had earned it.

For the entire journey, Hogstein was out for the count. Fumbling in my phrasebook, I asked to be dropped off a few blocks before his hotel; I didn't want him to see me when the driver had to wake him up and deposit him. Wandering through the city centre, I didn't really take in all the skyscraping blocks and monuments and churches. I just made a beeline for the nearest restaurant. Although the sign said 'Georgian Cuisine', it reminded me of Caesar Pizza with its fake plastic grapevine crawling over the ceiling. There was no pizza. But there was this boat-shaped cheesy flatbread with dough-handles and an egg cracked on top, so I got that, after showing my G.S.L. tattoo. It was called a *hatcha-pouri* and it was every bit as good as – maybe even better than – an anchovy pizza. Hogstein was off my hands. But somewhere out there, among the crowds rushing past with their upturned collars and shawls and cigarettes, squinting through the snow, was Swirly Ben.

What was so special about these spatula

necklaces? It seemed safe now to examine them closely. One was Professor Peshkova's. The other was Kirill's. Kirill! Had he even boarded the train of doom at St Petersburg? Or had he been saved by getting stuck in the queue for the toilets?

In shape and size, the necklaces were exactly the same. But . . . I picked them up and rubbed them. The actual spatula bit . . . the square on the end with the grooves in between. The *grooves* were different. And it was more than just the width of the gaps. Along them were all these little nicks.

I saw it now. If you just looked at these grooves, and ignored the rest of the spatula, they resembled the nicks of a key. A key to unlock the Brillerge egg cups, surely! I rang Princess.

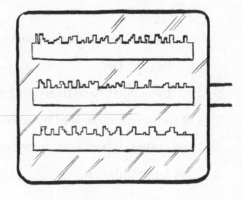

'I was just about to call you, Colin,' she said.

Colin. That was weird – why was she calling me by my real name? It sounded so distant, somehow.

'Are you aware that there's been another major breach of security?'

'Er . . . what's going on?'

'You tell me.'

'I don't know what you're talking about, Princess.'

'What I'm talking about, pizza-head, is that I received a phone call today, on a HIGHLY CONFIDENTIAL NUMBER THAT NOBODY SHOULD EVER KNOW, from, of all people, *your sister.*'

A bit of *hatcha-pouri* somersaulted inside me.

'I'm . . . I'm . . .'

'I shouldn't have to remind you that this kind of indiscretion *can* lead to prosecution at the G.S.L. law courts, where your membership may or may not be withdrawn.'

'But Princess . . . she broke into my secret office . . . how was I to –'

'You're on very thin ice, Anchovy. *Very* thin. Over and out.'

Alicia. The little . . . I didn't even want to source the fruit pastilles now. She had just crossed a serious line.

Now, more than ever, I wanted to go home. I didn't want to go out *there*. A worker in a crane was hacking giant icicles off buildings, before they fell off and speared passers-by. Trucks ploughed snow into great dirty mountains. Mascots gave out flyers, dressed as pandas or Pokémons or those food-headed characters I'd seen in St Petersburg. Everyone was rushing, plunging into the warm Metro stations. How was I supposed to find Swirly Ben in a city of (from one of Hogstein's worksheets) 13 million people? He didn't even have his distinctive rug of beard any more. And what the crust was I going to do about Alicia?

The food-headed mascots were calling it a day.
I didn't blame them. I watched this little tomato
guy in a black tailcoat. He was taking off his big
red head. A mosaic of snow mottled his features –
but I recognised him. That upturned nose. That
scarecrow hair. Those beady eyes. Justin. AKA
Juice Box. My nemesis had come to Moscow.

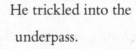

He trickled into the
underpass.

Just seen Justin! I
typed to Princess. **Tailing
him.**

I threw on my coat
and headed out. A gaggle
of army cadets screened
me as Justin passed the
kiosks. He came up
onto the ring road: eight

lanes of traffic roaring through the slush. Then he crossed a square with a statue of a man with a billowy beard. Finally, he headed to a grand building with classical pillars, and slinked through another mammoth doorway. He barely checked if he was being followed. No wonder he never made it past the G.S.L.'s auditions. The entrance was hung with posters of ballet dancers and a sign saying 'The Bolshoi Theatre'.

Inside, I stood out like . . . well, a British pizza detective at a Russian ballet. Justin, who had somehow magically disposed of his tomato head, blended in more with his black tailcoat. I followed as he climbed some stairs, edged along a landing and wormed through a trapdoor into a ventilation shaft. A crew of waiters were clearing up glasses. I peeked into the dark theatre. Presumably, the interval had just ended. Applause was ebbing. An orchestra swelled. People in turquoise were prancing onstage. There was a gentle cough at my side. A waiter with a silver platter was offering me an open smoked salmon sandwich. A bottle of champagne, the size of a traffic cone, concealed his face. I took the sandwich. I only saw a ring on his little finger, as he whipped away the tray and left. The sandwich was garnished in some kind of herb. Dill? The fronds had been carefully arranged to spell out the letters:

This can't have been sent by the G.S.L. I would've just got a message on the pizza watch. Or the waiter would've shown me their badge. Or asked to see mine.

'Avoid the Metro'? Why? I couldn't worry about rush hour crowds now. Justin's trapdoor beckoned.

I had to find out what he was up to.

On my belly, I slid into the ventilation shaft, holding my breath. Eventually a shard of light pierced through. I heard his snivelling voice. I crawled to the opening. Below was one of the strangest sights I have ever witnessed. There was Justin, talking to a pile of *giant rats*. Well, I should be specific – it was a pile of giant rat *costumes*. And massive rag-dolls. And life-sized wooden soldiers. And pieces of fake pirate ship. And broken ladders. Trapped under this groaning mountain of eerie costumes and props, cast in shadow, lay a man in a rat costume, struggling for air. Justin took the big rat head and twisted it. The person underneath gasped.

'Still no idea about these egg cups, Mr Kitov?' sneered the pest. 'Hmmm? What's that?'

Mr Kitov? Wait . . .

'Come on, spit it out!'

Kitov . . . I recalled the menu in Fryer Tuck's: that was Kirill's surname. And that face – the swoosh of silvery hair, the dark circles under the squirrelly eyes . . . it was Kirill's dad!

'Oh, you want something to drink, do you, Mr Kitov?' Justin sneered again. 'Here you go.'

He brought out a juice carton and offered him the straw. But as the trapped pianist tried to slurp it, Justin squashed the carton against his face. Purple gunk oozed out and onto the rat costume. I couldn't purée-gun Justin from here. There was every chance I'd take down Kirill's dad instead. But I shouldn't have gasped. Gasps are never good in ventilation shafts.

'Who's there?' Justin bawled. 'Who's there, I said!'

I waited. He waited. Mr Kitov probably waited too.

'Maybe it was just another dirty little rat, Mr

Kitov. You'd like that, wouldn't you? Lying down here with some *real* rats to keep you company. Well, time for your nap, Mr Kitov.'

He stuck the big rat head back on the poor guy. Then he began punching numbers into his phone with those stubby, juice-stained fingers. The voice that answered was painfully audible. And painfully familiar.

'Hello, darling?'

'He's in the Metro, Miss Heidi,' said the little pest.

'Who is, child? That silly little Swirly Bun?'

'Yeah. At Ploshad Revolutsi. Been sitting there all day, Billy no mates.'

'Wonderful, darling. Like a sitting duck.'

I wanted to message the team, but I had no time. That gruesome worm began climbing towards the shaft. I shimmied out like I'd never shimmied before. Hurtling down the staircase, knocking past the ballet-goers, I bounded out of the foyer and back across the square. I saw the giant 'M' sign for the Metro, glowing like an ember. Crowds were bottlenecking at a set of silver doors, which swung like the arms of a pinball machine. I squeezed through the bodies to what I presumed was a ticket machine, tapped the screen, got what I hoped was a ticket, and shoved through the turnstiles. Then I nearly fell over with giddiness. I was on the longest, steepest escalator imaginable. It seemed to be rumbling us down to the centre of the earth. The Moscow Metro. I've talked about the winter palace and its wow factor. This – compared to London's hamster-tunnel equivalent – wasn't far off a palace in itself. A procession of chandeliers melted out of the dimness. The hall below was decked in mosaics, frilled with gold and exploding red stars. Torrents of people splurged forth from their marble anthills. I followed the signs to 'Ploshad Revolutsi'. Finally, I came into another hall with gloomy archways, burnt-red and lead-grey. Guarding these were brass statues with tree-trunk limbs, carrying rifles and baskets and sheaves of corn. One had a dog, whose nose everyone rubbed, as if for good luck. Years of this had made it gleam like a beacon. By this dog was a ledge. On this ledge was a figure, shrouded in balloons. No one was buying any. On his lap lay a sheet of greaseproof paper. On this, a snail-shaped pastry.

All was not lost.

I had found Swirly Ben.

Chapter 14

I sat by the balloons and dug out the spatulas. A gnarled hand tucked away the pastry. Then it handed me seven balloons. The cloud of balloons shifted, surrounding us both. Beard-free, there were shades of Hogstein about the guy. If you left Hogstein in the bath all day and he'd turned into a mega-prune. Not an image I want in my head. Anyway, here he was, Swirly Ben, in the Moscow Metro, alive and well. Ish. Without fanfare or explanation, he passed me his spatula. The trio was complete.

'Where is the Brillerge, Swirly Ben? I'm here

to help you, I promise.'

Now was the time, I thought, for a simple, *normal* answer. I thought wrong. His eyes misted over and he began to chant.

'Find the house where nations sleep,

Where no one stays and nothing keeps,

Where our forebears once awoke,

In a chimney without smoke.'

How did this guy get anything done? Still, if there's one thing I've learnt from G-pops, it's that you need to be patient with old people. Very patient. I looked at him searchingly.

'And where's that, Swirly Ben?'

He was silent. Expressionless. It reminded me of Hogstein, when we asked him questions like 'But why did the Vikings bother coming to Britain?' or 'Did Henry the Eighth really need six wives?' or 'Sir, sir, why did you say the peasants were revolting?' He was also silent at times like these.

Also expressionless. Partly, he was just stunned by our ignorance. But also, he wanted us to work it out for ourselves. I pictured the old warbler, going heavy on the cheese soufflé in his posh hotel. Wait a minute! Posh hotel. A place that people visit from all over the world.

'A house (kind of) that sleeps nations.'

Swirly Ben – did he mean a posh hotel?

'Swirly Ben, do you mean a posh hotel?'

Still showing about as much emotion as a goldfish, he nodded.

I was breaking through the riddle force field! But then my watch began to beep. I ignored it. This wasn't a time for interruptions!

'The Hotel Metropole?'

The goldfish face nodded again.

Beeeeeeeeeeeep!

More cold-shouldering from Colin.

'Inside . . . the chimney?'

Another nod.

'Will you meet me there?'

A third nod.

Beeeeeeeeeeeeeeeeeeeeep!

I had so many questions – like, where was the keyhole for this spatula key? And how do you access a posh chimney in a posh hotel? And why couldn't you have just said 'Hotel Metropole' to begin with? But there wasn't time. There were two reasons for this. First, Swirly Ben passed me the balloon cloud, picked up his stick, and vanished into the crowd. Second, the archways of Ploshad Revolutsi began to echo with a *BANG! BANG! BANG!*

I saw my rookie mistake. Never ignore a long beep on the pizza watch. I grabbed the purée gun. But this wasn't gunfire. It was seven, eight, nine, ten, eleven, twelve balloons popping. The cloud dispersed, the helium squealing. I stared into the beady eyes of Justin. He was holding a needle.

'Didn't get an invite to your balloon party,
Anchy . . . where did Granddad go?'

I shrugged.

'Ooooh, not feeling very helpful, are we,
Anchy Wanch? But I'm guessing from your chat
that he's done one to Hotel Metropole. Funny
how the old codger spotted the danger before you
did – and you're an actual G.S.L. detective. What
a joke!'

This kid was asking for a molten tomato-ing.
But before I could unleash the purée, a chunky
policeman stepped out from behind a statue.
He had a moustache like a coughed-up furball.
He reeked of what I can only describe as eau
de ashtray. And his sniffer dog was substantially
wolfier than average. Glitterpuff.

'Fancy meeting you here, son,' said Constable
Pudders, pointing his klashni-mabob gun – or

whatever it was called – at me. 'Be a good lad now and come this way.'

What else could I do? At least Swirly Ben had evaded capture. Again.

The platforms were lit with the glare of an approaching train's headlights. I quickly noshed my edible notebook. Delicious.

'Hands up,' Pudders fuzz-mumbled. He'd probably been waiting his whole life to say that. Again, what else could I do?

'Don't think you'll be needing this little gizmo.' Justin took my pizza watch and threw it under the train. To add insult to injury, he also took my purée gun, phone and wallet.

'Oh, you made it sooooo easy for us, Anch,' sniggered Justin. 'Even that weedy pianist's son put up more of a fight!'

'What have you done with Kirill, you little fluff-sack?'

'Woah, *Anchy*, baby!' He beckoned me in closer. 'I wouldn't be so lippy if I had a big ol' gun poking in my back and an even bigger dog licking his chops.'

Pudders chuckled. Not that it sounded like a chuckle, with all those cigarettes scratching at his windpipe. Justin delved into my trench coat.

'Yes, mate!' He had found the necklaces. 'These make a tidy little set, don't they?'

'Justin,' I said bitterly. 'It was you who rigged the houseboat, wasn't it?'

He gave me a smarmy grin.

'Ha! Yeah . . . your mate Swirly Ben saw me prowling and gave me the slip that time as well.' He toyed with the necklaces. 'But I still had time to set up a nice little crossbow. And a nice little explosive. Not bad eh?'

Just looking at him made me queasy. It was all hitting home now.

'And it was *you* who phoned the school and tried to pin the fire on me, wasn't it?'

Justin didn't even blink.

'Ten out of ten, Anchy! Hahaha!'

Prodding me with the Kalashnikov (I knew I'd get it eventually), the gruesome twosome marched me to the escalator. I was in front, Pudders and Glitterpuff behind, Juice Box at the rear. By the time we reached the top, I knew I needed a plan. I realised now that Justin had heard me in the theatre. He had sent me to the Metro. And now he knew all about the Hotel Metropole. How wrong I had been to doubt him. I had even been warned! I hate it when villains do this. You do all the hard work, sweating away for three very elusive spatula keys, find out where some priceless jewelled egg cups are stashed, then they swoop in and take all the glory. Other passengers bustled past. All going about their peaceful daily lives. There was a mother taking her daughter to a violin lesson. A slim guy in a tracksuit, perhaps off to football practice. A smooching couple. A granny with cat baskets. They gave me dirty looks. They probably thought *I* was the criminal, being frogmarched by a policeman, a sniffer dog and the ferret-faced Juice Box.

A vicious *hiss* sliced the air. It was the cats in the baskets. At least they were on my side. Glitterpuff thrashed. My lightbulb moment arrived. If you so much as breathed the word 'cats' to G-pops' dog, Dinnergloves (especially if you drew out the 's' – *catsssssss*), he went ballistic, running in circles and barking at the sky, despite being a sweet dog for 99% of the time. So imagine what would happen if I showed a cat to Glitterpuff, a thoroughly nasty dog for 100% of the time. I could see the top of the escalator. Whatever had to happen, it had to happen now. Justin had wrecked my watch. But he didn't have my glue-gun cufflinks. I sprayed the

steps in glue and sneakily opened the cat baskets.
There was a *WHUMP WHUMP WHUMP* as
Unkle Pudders stacked it and got glued to the floor.
Glitterpuff, as much as he was salivating over a
Colin sandwich, couldn't resist two uncaged cats.

YEEOOOWWWWWW went the cats.

RRAAAAARRGH went the wolf.

'COME BACK!' added Justin.

To add to the confusion, two genuine police
dogs joined in. There was a hairy wolfy whirlpool,
Pudders got trampled, and I started to run.
But I froze at what I saw in the ticket hall. The
Tangerine Terror.

'Stop that boy!!' she wailed. Pudders took off his
boots and tumbled in his socks. Glitterpuff ditched
the cats. I vaulted a barrier, crowd-surfed a sea of
hats and leapt onto the escalator going back down.
As it was rammed, my only option was a very
naughty one. I slid down the handrail. A train was

pulling in.

Glitterpuff was

gaining on me, a snarling torpedo.

RARRRRRRGH! RAAARGHH!

RAAAARRRGGHH!

I flew up the platform and onto a carriage. I like to think the doors squished Glitterpuff's horrible snout, but I couldn't be sure. The train rattled off into the darkness.

Chapter 15

For the umpteenth time this trip, I was an absolute sweat-fest. Being sardined in with Moscow's heftiest didn't help. Thankfully I was squidged up against the end door. I scanned the carriage for Pudders and Justin. Something glimmered in the adjoining carriage. It was an emerald ring, worn by – who? They were blocked from view. My brain began to sting. I *knew* that hand. I closed my eyes, the image whirling inside my head. I caught it. The waiter at the Bolshoi! Slender and pale, holding the tray, with the warning in dill lettering, and the ring on his little finger . . . but no matter how much I craned my neck, I couldn't see the owner of this hand. And now we were stopping at Arbatskaya station. The man with the emerald ring got out and joined the crowd. I only caught the back of him, clad in a magenta tracksuit. I followed the stampede through a gilded hall and onto another escalator. The man in the tracksuit weaved on up. When I reached the top, he was heading down a yellow-tiled passage towards the clattering turnstiles. I charged out. The night chill prickled my skin. Tracksuit Man was receding up more steps, past another beardy statue and through the doors of yet another towering edifice. The architecture in Moscow made me feel like an ant. This whopper had 'BIBLIOTEKA' carved into it. Which I remembered from Camillo's phrase book meant 'library'.

Opening the door required superhuman strength. Now, Rufflington Library isn't a bad

little place. A reddish-brown building with my
favourite books in one corner, playgroups in
another, oddballs using the toilet. But it seemed
a bit of a joke compared to this library. Rippling
marble columns shot to the ceiling like gold-
topped skyscrapers. Busts of Russian writers looked
down on a green sea of reading lights. Along a
landing, old men played chess or took newspapers
from wooden drawers, nibbling cherry pies and
slurping coffee from brown plastic cups. And
there was Tracksuit Man, slipping through some
humungous doors. He was gone when I reached
them, but I could hear his footsteps, pattering
down some stairs. I followed. With each staircase,
the ceilings grew lower. There were fewer people
here. The ceiling was too low for most adults to
stand up straight. Then the landings became barely
tall enough for even me. Tracksuit Man kept
on spiralling down. Finally, I heard a soft voice

whisper, 'Chukrovsky . . .'

Chukrovsky . . . a password? The name of a guard to a hidden door?

The stairwell ended. There was a bust of some cheery old man with a bulbous nose.

'Chukrovsky!' I called.

Nothing.

I tried again, louder. 'Chuk-rov-sky!!'

Still nothing.

I paced down the wood-panelled passage. G.S.L. caterer detectives are trained from an early age to run a basic check over panelled walls (referred to in the manual as an HPP – Hidden Panel Procedure), as they are classic places for secret doors. Too classic, sometimes. I went to the bust.

'Chukrovsky?' I tried again. Even if it was a special password, it wasn't working. Spitefully, I flicked the bulbous nose. And *bing!* The wall began to move. I stepped through the gap and sneezed. I was in a book-lined, hexagonal room, swimming with dust. A grubby painting hung above an ink-stained desk. Seated at this was someone well-versed in the art of spinning away in a swivel chair.

'You have just made me break one of the most sacred rules for retired ex-Presidents,' purred the voice. The chair spun dramatically. He'd obviously been practising.

'Master Key!'

'Good evening, Anchovy.'

Of the many shocks I'd had on this trip, this was the biggest. My ex-mentor, Master Key, sushi chef and expert in infiltration. The person who had recruited me at the very beginning. I stared into his almond-shaped face, one eye blue, the other brown. He had changed out of the tracksuit and into his signature silk dressing gown. The emerald ring twinkled in the lamplight..

'Is it illegal for you to contact me?' I asked.

'Absolutely.' He spoke gravely. 'For those departed from the Golden Spatula League, it is strictly forbidden to communicate with current catering detectives. Once you leave, you *leave*.'

From his dressing-gown pocket, he took out a small tin, and applied some peachy face cream to a pimple.

'And by the way, Anchovy, I really think you ought to listen when you get a warning as gilt-edged as that.'

'Do you mean the dill lettering on the smoked salmon sandwich?'

'They were chives, but yes, that is the sandwich in question. By the way, I'm sorry about your singed eyebrows.'

'Thanks.'

He brought out a gold teapot. A fruity aroma undulated through the dust.

'Tea?'

'Do we have time?'

'There is always time for tea.'

'It's just that Kirill's dad is being held hostage in a rat costume under the Bolshoi Theatre.'

'I see.' He brought out writing paper, a pot of purple ink and a fountain pen, and began scrawling. 'I shall help you make arrangements.'

Whether it was tea or the Elixir of Life, after a

few sips I felt like a new detective.

'Master Key . . . what are you doing here? I thought you'd be on holiday forever now.'

'I'm reading.' He smiled. 'During those years in the G.S.L., there were so many books that I never got around to, so now I'm making up for lost time. I'm on the Russian classics at the moment. Have you heard of *War and Peace*?'

'Don't. Who's the guy with the bulbous nose out there?'

'Chukrovsky? A famous children's writer. He has a wonderful poem about washing, which I thoroughly recommend.'

I sniffed my pits. What was he trying to say? I took a sip of tea but spurted it out.

'Lady Grey. Rather fruity, I should've warned you.'

'It's not . . . the tea . . .' I choked. 'It's that painting behind you.'

Those children in sailor suits and smocks . . . the flags on the pier . . . I couldn't believe what I was seeing. It was a reproduction of the torn photograph on Swirly Ben's houseboat! But that wasn't the weirdest part. The children's faces had been *scratched out.*

'What is this place?' I said, looking around. 'And why have the children's faces been gouged out? Who are they?'

'You are in a long-lost archive for the Associated Red Spoons. When they came to power, they removed and vandalised all images associated with the Golden Spatula League. This room has been sealed for decades. No one knows about it – except you and me.'

I didn't bother asking how he got in. I knew that Master Key could get in anywhere.

Squinting at the painting, I saw the telling detail. Something that Swirly Ben's grainy photograph hadn't captured. Each of those children wore the same piece of jewellery: a necklace with a mini spatula.

'Are these the Russian G.S.L.?'

'The very same. Otherwise known as the magic quartet.'

Quartet?

'Wait . . .' I said, 'there's a *fourth* key out there?'

Master Key poured out more tea, the steam curling in blue-grey tendrils.

'Are you aware, Anchovy, of the most common place to find a lost key?'

'Er . . . no.'

'Your pocket.'

Well, that was patronising.

'Er, yeah . . . I don't think so,' I said.

'Why not just check?'

I went through my trouser pockets, then through the trench coat. Anything in there I placed on the

desk. Some napkins. The paper bag from the *pishki*.
My ticket from the Church of the Spilled Blood. My
ticket from the Hermitage. My coat tag from the
cloakroom when I forgot the fur coat. Hogstein's
worksheet, folded and dog-eared. The Russian
phrase book. A shiny gum wrapper. A toothpick
from the Georgian restaurant. What had Swirly Ben
said about these keys? I closed my eyes and thought
of his riddles. There was the one about the snail and
the fish – no . . . The winter palace . . . wait.

Shed the fleece and leave behind.

Take a number always moving.

'Holy pepperoni!' I shouted. 'The coat tag!'

I picked it up: red, plastic, smaller than a bank
card but thicker, with a hole for looping over a coat
hook, and a Tippexed white number: *579. A number
always moving.* This was an item forever changing
hands, never staying in one place. But unless you
forfeited your coat, it would never really leave that

place. I rattled it and heard a tiny
rumble. A slit ran down the side.
Digging a nail in, I prised it open.
A fine chain had been wound
into a spiral. And on the end
hung the golden spatula.

'Wooah!' I could see
that the nicks between the gaps were
different to the others. It was a unique key.

'How many of these things are there?'

'This, I promise you, Anchovy, is the final one.
It's unlike you to miss the obvious, but can you
spot the main difference between that painting and
Swirly Ben's sepia photograph?'

It was obvious. Embarrassingly obvious. Swirly
Ben's torn photo only showed *three* of the four
children. Because, duh-brain Colin, it was torn.

'The fourth detective,' said Master Key, 'is
curiously absent from the G.S.L. history books. His

name was Denis Danish. Each of the quartet was given a spatula key as custodians of the Brillerge. Swirly Ben, the sole survivor, managed to keep hold of his.'

'And one sent theirs to Kirill's ancestor?'

'Correct. Her name was Claire Éclair.'

'Then another, discovered by Professor Peshkova . . .'

'Correct again – most probably that would've belonged to Detective Charlotka.'

'And the fourth, Denis Danish, managed to *hide* his,' I said.

'Precisely. I believe it's his granddaughter who now works in the Hermitage cloakrooms.'

I passed the necklace to Master Key, stunned. With his blue eye, he examined the nicks.

'Let me tell you a thing or two

about keys, Anchovy. Among experts, this particular model is known as an Orfevre '86. Delicate yet durable, it relies on a flashy though impractical system, which largely went out of fashion in the 1920s. In essence, the Orfevre '86 deploys multiple rows of interlocking teeth. Rather than doors or drawers, they tend to be implemented on clamps or brackets. Holding devices. Most importantly, however, they operate on the basis of synchronicity between multiple users.'

He was getting all Hogsteiny on me.

'What does that mean?'

'It means, Anchovy, that the Brillerge egg cups are in a vault or safe that can only be opened by these four keys turning at the *exact same second*.'

Relief poured over me in bucket-loads.

'You mean that, however much Heidi's gang huff and puff, it's impossible to open the vault without this last key?'

'Exactly. Even if they – or anyone – actually knows where the vault is. I can only tell you about keys.'

It was my moment to shine. Like when I'm watching a game show with G-pops and he knows the answer to every question, except for the million-pound jackpot, which is the only one I do know.

'It's in the Hotel Metropole,' I said. 'Hidden by Swirly Ben when he worked there as a pastry chef.'

He sat up. 'I always knew you had something special, Anchovy!'

'How far away is the Metropole?'

'How good are you at throwing stones?'

'I'm okay.'

'Well, if you happened to be exceedingly good, and bunged a stone from here, you'd possibly break a window.' He resumed scrawling with the fountain pen. 'By the way, does Heidi know about the vault in the Metropole?'

'Yep, unfortunately . . .'

'Does she know whereabouts it is?'

'Justin heard me talking to Swirly Ben about a chimney. But I'm guessing there's probably more than one in there . . .'

Master Key sighed. 'The place is simply *heaving* with chimneys, Anchovy. But if anyone can find the right one, it's you.'

He handed me an envelope.

'Ask for Lyosha at reception and give him this. I think he's still working there – a good sort, a bit quiet, rather an undramatic G.S.L. career. Until now. He will alert the London branch as to your whereabouts, and you can go from there.'

'You're not coming with me?'

'I'll escort you there, of course, my friend. But I cannot participate in what is strictly a G.S.L. operation. I've broken enough rules just by contacting you.'

At another time, I might have enjoyed the walk there. We passed a fairy-tale castle, topped with red stars, which I think Master Key called the 'gremlin'. Then I glimpsed a famous-looking church with kaleidoscopic onion-domes. There was a square that was supposedly 'red', even though it looked pretty grey-and-brown to me. Fur-hatted soldiers stamped around as tourists took selfies. All very impressive. But my thoughts were elsewhere. A sickly pink light was spilling from the Metropole. A black car oiled up, snowflakes falling in the headlights. Master Key shook my hand.

'This is it, Anchovy. Remember, you never saw me.' He smiled. '*Oodachi*.'

Ooo-what?

He got into the car, which slid silently away.

Time to find some egg cups.

Chapter 16

I stood out like a stranded anchovy. What with all the chandeliers, plush carpets, marble counter, snooty doormen and designer suitcases, I had to wonder: how had Hogstein been allowed in with *that* bonnet? I read the word *Lyosha* / Лйоша on a gold badge on a bored boy. He wore a dark green jacket and was piling up hatboxes with all the urgency of a snail on holiday.

'Lyosha?'

He stirred from his sleepwalking. '*Kto tee?*'

I gave him Master Key's letter. He tilted his

head, raised his eyebrows, and beckoned me through a staff door. 'Please, the toe.'

I've often thought a finger tattoo would've been easier. I took off my trainer and sock. Lyosha was satisfied with the G.S.L. badge of recognition.

'Lyosha,' I asked, 'has a woman with pigtails and a dog that looks like a wolf checked in?'

'Ah . . .' he said dreamily, searching his brain. (I mean, how many people match that description?!) 'Yes . . . yes, there was such a woman! She was very rude to us.'

'She's like that with everyone. Was there a boy with her? Tall, dark, with fidgety hands?'

'Yes!' He was quicker this time.

'And a bulky man who needed a shave?'

'Yes!'

'And another, more annoying boy?'

'Yes! He complained that we do not have enough ice-cream toppings in the hotel. But we have twelve! Which I think is –'

'Yes, yes, that's all I need to know,' I cut in. 'They're all here. Can you phone the London Headquarters, please?'

He pulled a secret phone from what looked like a bread bin, spinning his finger in the old-fashioned dial.

'*Aureum in spatha est, vivat spatha,*' he said slowly. 'London *pazhulasta* . . . ahem . . . Good evening. That is to say, good afternoon. Please may I speak with Princess Skewer?'

I pictured the commotion in the labyrinth under Fryer Tuck's greasy diner.

'Tell her it is Lyosha Levin, Moscow Metropole, please.'

He finally got Princess and explained the situation. She didn't need to be put on loudspeaker. There was a lot of 'fluffing this' and 'fluffing that', which went over Lyosha's head. He passed me the receiver, which felt like a stick of dynamite.

'Yes?'

'Anchovy! Holy shish, where have you *been*?'

'I saw the ballet, took the Moscow Metro, and went to the library. I found out tha–'

'Anchovy, I couldn't care less about your cultural bonanza! Do you realise Kirill is missing? And Swirly Ben is missing? And now *three* spatulas are missing? And, up until recently, *you* were missing? What are you playing at?!'

'Kirill is in the hotel. Heidi Hyde High has him hostage.'

(Man, that was a tongue-twister.)

'I like the hotel part. The hostage part less so.'

'They also have the three spatula keys.'

'You really are a gift that keeps on giving, aren't you?'

'But wait . . . I have the fourth key.'

'There's *another* key?'

I explained about the fourth detective. The fourth key. The vault in the chimney. How it couldn't open without all four keys being turned at once. And that Swirly Ben was on his way.

'Where did you find this out?'

'Like I said, I went to the library.' I remembered my promise to Master Key. 'Also, you might want to send someone to the Bolshoi Theatre. Kirill's dad is trapped under a pile of rat costumes.'

'Hmmmmm . . .' She paused, weighing up the facts. 'While I'm not at *all* happy that you went AWOL, it seems like you have done some good work. Hold tight. I'm sending Anchka plus Camillo and the twins. Over and out.'

Eventually the troops arrived. Anchka wore a dark green Metropole eye patch. The twins had found some horrendous, fluorescent fur coats to match their hair. Camillo's nose was running like a tap. He wheeled in a suitcase, set up his little

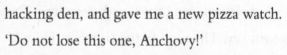

hacking den, and gave me a new pizza watch.

'Do not lose this one, Anchovy!'

'I didn't lose it, I was mugged!'

BEEP BEEP! BEEP BEEP! BEEP BEEP!

Princess's face appeared on five watch-screens.

'Okay, team. We've got a lot to do so we need everybody playing at the top of their game. Which means, twins, don't bicker; Lyosha, don't faff; Anchovy, don't go AWOL; and Camillo, please blow your nose. It looks like there's a colony of bats in there or something. Anchka, you're all good.'

Presumably she had started as she meant to go on.

'Here's what we're going to do. Lyosha: head to the Bolshoi. We need you to find a captured pianist.'

'There's a trapdoor on the landing,' I explained.

'The coast should be clear. After the trapdoor, you'll find the props and costumes room. In there you'll find a mountain of giant rat costumes. Kirill's dad is under it.'

Lyosha gulped like a bullfrog with a Strepsil.

'Just text us if you get stuck,' said Princess as he left. 'Anchovy: tell Anchka what you know about the vault.'

'Well,' I began, 'Swirly Ben worked here, right? So maybe we could start with a Hidden Panel Procedure in the kitchens?'

Anchka shook her head.

'Not possible, Anchovy. The kitchens have been renovated several times in this hotel. I know this from colleagues who used to work here.'

'I think we need more than a basic HPP, Anches,' said Princess.

'Okay,' I said, racking my brain. 'What would a pastry chef do in a hotel like this? I mean, any special routines, places he would've hung out in a lot?'

'We learnt in G.S.L. history books that he actually lived at the hotel,' said Anchka.

'Why?' I asked.

'Because pastry chefs get up at stupid o'clock, dough-brain,' said Princess.

'This is true,' said Anchka. 'But also at one time, some rooms here contained the Russian G.S.L. Headquarters before they were destroyed. And as Ulitka – *oy*, Swirly Ben – was a special case, they would need him staying here for emergencies.'

I got to the point.

'Where was his bedroom?'

'We don't have this kind of information.'

'Anchka, could you get some floor plans of the hotel?' I asked. 'One from today, one from 1917?'

'I will enquire about this. One moment, please.' She scuttled off.

'Not a bad shout, that,' said Princess. 'While we're waiting, Camillo, hack into Mr Hogstein's phone.'

'Okay, Princess. It will be tricky, the phone I think is from 2007 –'

'Just do it.'

Camillo got hacking.

'Anchovy, when he comes on, speak to Mr Hogstein and tell him you're back in the UK.'

The line was ringing.

'Yelena – or Yaconda – stand by to impersonate Anchovy's mum.'

Hogstein answered.

'Hello?'

'Oh hi, sir. It's Colin here. Just to say –'

'Kingsley! Where are you?'

'I'm home, sir. I'm back in Rufflington. So it's okay, sir, you can come back now.'

'Do you expect me to fall for that rot, Kingsley?!'

Princess readied the twins.

'I know what you are, young man! You're a devious little tearaway delinq–'

'Oh, Mr Hogstein?'

'Oh helloooo, Mrs Kingsley!'

The twins had it down to a tee. That super-polite, high-pitched, parents-evening voice. It was like my mum was actually there with us.

'Yes yes, quite an adventure. Well, Colin's back with us now, Mr Hogstein, yes yes. We're terribly sorry for the inconvenience caused to you and, of course, we'll be having strong words with Colin about all this.'

'All the same, I think we should meet to –'

Princess made a throat-slitting gesture.

'Goodbye, Mr Hogstein. We've got some customers we need to serve, sorry!'

'Camillo,' said Princess, 'what's the situation with Hogstein's flight?'

Camillo's hands were a blur on the keypad. 'Hmm, it says he has booked on the 17:35 flight from Moscow – soon he should be leaving the hotel.'

'Roger.'

Seriously, who was Roger?

Anchka came back with two rolled maps of the hotel. We unfurled them, past and present.

'*Vot!*' Anchka pointed to a narrow strip in the top right corner on the 1917 edition.

'What does it say?'

'It says "Sleeping Quarters for Kitchen Staff".'

I compared it the present version, then located the room nearest the chimney.

'Looks like we're heading to the attic.'

'Good work, Anches,' said Princess.

'Ah, Princess,' said Camillo. 'Maybe the CCTV as well?'

'Oh yeah, thanks Cam,' said Princess.

'What's that?' I asked Camillo.

'Simple procedure,' he said, as he always did for a mega-fiddly procedure. 'Like in the Uslizi archives in Rome, remember? I take down the CCTV and replace it with yesterday's footage. Now we will not be seen on the cameras.' I watched him in his hacking trance, spotlit by the screen's blue halo.

'Okay, twins,' said Princess. 'Yelena: find Hogstein. Yaconda: find Swirly Ben.'

The twins donned uniforms.

'Oh, and Yelena,' said Princess as they were leaving the cupboard, 'I don't want Hogstein using the corridors in case he bumps into Anchovy. Keep him in the buffet.'

'Should be easy. The blinis are incredible.'

'Next step: Anchka, find Heidi's room and prepare a tray of caviar and champagne.'

Anchka found the goods. Rather her than me.

'Camillo: a microphone inside the caviar tin, please. Also the tiniest, subtlest earpiece for Kirill.'

'One moment, Princess.'

He rummaged inside his suitcase and brought out a gleaming, pearl-sized earpiece. Room service was ready.

'In a few minutes, Anchka, you'll deliver this and establish communication with Kirill. Wait for my signal.'

Anchka looked unfazed. I hoped she had wolf-proof trousers.

'Okay, Anchovy and Camillo. Get a bag and pack a scalpel, steel ruler, a ton of cufflink glue, sponge, water – oh, and an iron. Then head to the attic. It's time for the main event.'

Chapter 17

A lift to the top, a maze of corridors, a cleaner's cupboard, a trapdoor, some lock-picking (Master Key would've breezed it) and we were in. Our flashlights zipped around. It was like underwater footage of a shipwreck: once grand, now all barnacled, lost in grey-green shadow. The original Russian G.S.L.'s Headquarters, caked in dust. We could make out the workbenches, the network of brass pipes, all those little drawers, just like the London HQ below Fryer Tuck's.

It would have been deathly
silent were it not for Princess on
the pizza watch.

'You up there, boys?'

We gave a thumbs-up.

'Tell me what you're looking at.'

I was actually looking at the
snot hanging out of Camillo's nose,
but this probably wasn't the right answer.

'It's a dusty old space full of rubbish.' (The attic,
not Camillo's nose.) 'The chimney has some boxes,
a rusty pram or something, plus a couple of old
wardrobes shoved up against it.'

'So move them.'

I don't remember the term 'removal man'
being on my G.S.L. contract. We heaved away the
wardrobes. The fireplace was sealed. And, more
worryingly . . .

'No keyholes.'

'Hmmm. Hang on a minute. Yaconda, is that you?'

'Hi Princess – just FYI, I found Swirly Ben in the reading room. I think it's him. He's behind a huge newspaper, gibbering.'

The old newspaper-shield trick. As I said, Swirly Ben kept it old-school.

'Stall him there for now. Yelena, how's Hogstein?'

'Inhaling the beef stroganoff.'

'Top work. Anchka, stand by. We'll need you in a sec. Boys, what's the wallpaper like in that attic?'

Why the décor question? I sent her a photo.

'As I thought. Late 80s, early 90s. It's coming off. Camillo, show Anchovy the wallpaper technique.'

So as well as removal men, we were apparently interior decorators. We hoisted a ladder to the chimney and Camillo unpacked our big bag of random objects.

'First we must prepare the wallpaper, Anchovy,' he said, and began to *iron* it.

'The steam will make this easier.'

He then ran the sponge and some hot water over it and, using the ruler and scalpel, cut a line where the paper met the ceiling. Then with a broad, flat blade he prised it gently off the wall.

'Why can't you just rip it off, Cam? That's going to take ages!'

'We cannot do this, Anchovy, because it must look like it did before. No one can know we came here.'

I held the ladder and watched him. He peeled the paper off slowly, as if yanking it off would sting the wall. Below the wallpaper was a wodge of amber-yellow newspaper. Still no keyholes. Camillo persevered. As carefully as before, he removed the newspapers and blew off the dust.

The dust would play havoc with his snot-stream, I thought.

'Aahhhh . . .' He sighed then suppressed a sneeze. 'It seems we are close. But there is a problem. Take a look.'

We swapped places. There were three keyholes at the top of the wall. Three keyholes, not four. We peeled off a lower section of wallpaper. No keyholes there. Then another, on the side of the chimney. Still no keyholes. Then the other side, until the chimney was bare. Still – you guessed it – no keyholes.

'What do you think, Anchovy?'

I studied the three keyholes. They were positioned in a triangle, like this:

But what shape would a fourth keyhole, added above this, make? A diamond. To mirror the G.S.L. logo. Swirly Ben's riddle in the Church of the Spilled Blood came back to me:

The diamond's top is last in line.

He wasn't so loopy after all. I knocked on the ceiling. It echoed as if I'd knocked on cardboard. The fourth keyhole was above it. But this was looking impossible. First we'd have to get Kirill – Kirill, who wasn't even G.S.L.-trained – to steal the three keys. Then we'd have to somehow remove the fake ceiling. And maybe sledgehammer the chimney apart to actually get to the vault once we'd unclamped it from the inside. The cogs in my head were hurting. But they were trying to clank into gear.

Princess buzzed in.

'Any leads, you two?'

I explained about the fourth keyhole and the fake ceiling. Princess took it in, breathing heavily.

'Listen, we can't bulldoze any walls or ceilings. And we can't get Kirill to steal the keys. Even an apprentice couldn't do that. And Heidi won't fall for any more sedated snacks.'

My brain-cogs were trundling.

'So basically,' she went on, 'there are three key holes that we can't even touch.'

I had it.

'No,' I said. 'But *they* can.'

Chapter 18

'I like the cut of your jib,' said Princess. 'It's a juicy plan, Anchovy – but I'm going to make one adjustment. Which might mean you get a teeny-weeny bit cold.'

I shot Camillo a look.

A wavering beep announced Lyosha. He appeared on our watch-screens, propping up a giddy Mr Kitov.

'I have here the very delicate pianist.'

We whooped at his news.

'Amazing!'

'Excellent!'

'*Bravo!*'

'*Atleechna!*'

'There is a G.S.L. shuttle in the theatre café, Princess,' advised Anchka. 'It goes straight here.'

'Perfect, Anchka. In the meantime, head to the Monte Carlo suite with the bugged caviar.'

Back in Lyosha's cupboard/Camillo's hacking den, we studied the monitor. Anchka knocked at Heidi's lair. A grainy apparition answered the door. That loping gait, that black floppy hair, those squirrelly eyes: Kirill. It was hard to see if he was under gunpoint or wolf-point. You wouldn't bet against it. From within came blinding flashes, as Heidi took a ton of selfies. Kirill took the tray. And then Anchka did something incredible. She grabbed him by the ears and planted a big wet kiss on his cheek! Kirill went turbo-beetroot. As Anchka left, Heidi hollered, 'What are you doing, you wretched boy?'

Kirill touched his ear. I saw what Anchka had done.

'Kirill!' I said.

'Er . . . hello?' His voice was low, stealthy, confused.

'Kirill, this is Colin – I mean, Mark Anchovy. We're going to get you out of there. My colleague has just inserted a special earpiece.'

Kirill nodded, sheepishly.

'What is the matter with you, boy?' snapped Heidi.

'Kirill,' I said. 'Your Brillerge egg cups are in a vault in this hotel. But we'll need you to help. Instead of saying "yes", just sniff. For "no", cough. Are you okay?'

Sniff sniff.

'They haven't set Glitterpuff on you yet?'

Cough.

'You don't want to strangle Justin already?'

Ambiguous noise.

'Have Pudders and co. been knocking at any chimneys yet?'

Sniff.

Uh-oh.

'Have they talked about going to the attic?'

Cough.

In the background, we heard Heidi snatch the caviar and champagne. She didn't gobble it up right away.

'Ooooh, darling . . . complimentary champagne – wait a minute. I'm not falling for that poisonous filth again!' She was obviously having a painful memory of the train stunt.

'Justin, darling, would you care for a spot of caviar?'

'I'd eat some raspberry ripple ice cream if you had it.'

'Be a good boy now, darling, and try this caviar

for me. You don't want to make Glitterpuff cross, do you?'

Justin must've gulped it down. Some minutes passed.

'Oh, perhaps it's all fine . . .' cooed Heidi. I guessed Justin hadn't passed out. Shame.

'Stop stuffing yourself, you greedy little brat!'

There was a *nom-nom-nom* as she lost herself in the caviar.

'Kirill,' I said, 'here's the plan. Pretend that you've known all along about the Brillerge, that Swirly Ben told you, and now you're finally telling them. Got it?'

Sniff sniff.

'Good. Once you've done that, you're going to lead those mugs to the attic. Go to the top floor, by the cleaner's cupboard, then up through a trapdoor. The lock's already been picked, but pretend to pick it to keep up appearances. Princess Skewer will talk you through everything once you get there. All clear so far?'

Sniff sniff.

'No objections?'

Cough.

With all this sniffing and coughing, Heidi's gang might have worried about catching the flu from Kirill. At any rate, we saw him bravely leading the goon squad along the corridor. Glitterpuff padded next to him, eyeing his ankles. Then there was Heidi, twirling the spatula keys. Justin trotted behind. Pudders was last, with a sledgehammer and crowbar.

Anchka joined us back in Lyosha's cupboard.

'Well played, Anchka,' said Princess. 'Love scenes are always tricky. Twins: how's Mr Ben and the Hog?'

'Having a nap,' said Yaconda.

'Moving on to the cheese and crackers,' said Yelena.

Princess gave a thumbs-up.

'Camillo and Anchovy: wrap up warm and pack a bag for Basic Burglary Level 4.'

At least she didn't say 'Advanced Burglary Level 6'.

Camillo joke-saluted.

'Kirill, it's Princess here. Have you got Heidi and the gang to the cleaner's cupboard?'

Sniff sniff.

'Well done, great work. Now, I want you to really take your time with that lock. Just slow it right down. Anchka, once Kirill's got them inside, go back and stand *outside* the cleaner's cupboard on the top floor. Anchovy, Camillo, head to the roof.'

We took another plush maze to another lonely spot in the sprawling hotel. Camillo deactivated the alarm and we left the top floor via the fire exit.

The Metropole's roof was carpetted with snow. My face felt numb. Camillo's snot-stream was in full flow. We trudged to the chimney, checking on the plan. Camillo unpacked something that looked part-laser, part-saw, plus a harness, cables and some suction pads.

'Are you up there?' said Princess.

'Yep,' I said, and muttered, 'I hope it's nice and warm in Fryer Tuck's.'

Petty, I know.

'Right. Camillo, get to work on the chimney pots.'

Camillo's laser-saw must've stood out a mile as it snaked around the chimney. In addition there were sparks, staging their own firework display for all the world to see.

'Anchovy, help me take this off.'

As if he had just lopped off a choc-ice, the top of the chimney fell into our arms, almost crushing us.

We dumped it on the snow. Why join a gym if you can join the G.S.L.? I shone the flashlight into the opening.

'What do you see?' said Princess.

'There's a casket or box, like a briefcase, down there,' I said.

'Maybe we can tie some cables to it,' said Camillo.

'True,' I added, leaning further in, 'but it's clamped in place. I'm guessing from the *outside* of the chimney, below the roof, but above the fake ceiling. If that makes sense.'

'Kind of,' said Princess. 'Camillo, laser an Anchovy-sized hole in the roof, please.'

More lasering, more sparks. At least they provided some warmth. When the hole had stopped smouldering, Camillo buckled the harness onto me. He tied one end of the cable to the chimney, the other end to me, and lowered me through the hole. I lay in the tiny space below the roof, above the fake ceiling. There was the fourth keyhole. So far, so Tom Cruise. I took out the spatula key.

'I'm in, Princess. Ready to go.'

'Good. Listen up, team,' said Princess. 'It all comes down to this. One mistake and we're fluffed. Kirill: you need to get Pudders to bash out the old fireplace. Then you'll need to get Pudders, Justin and Heidi to open the three keyholes. You should *sneeze* when their keys are turning. Then stand inside the chimney and hold on to the casket as tightly as you can. Got that?'

Sniff sniff.

'Anchovy, when you hear the sneeze, turn the key. Camillo, when *you* hear the sneeze, pull out the casket through the chimney, along with Kirill. I'll talk you through the next steps from there. Anchka: at the sneeze, lock the door and call the police. I want them sealed in there. Twins, get a taxi for Swirly Ben and a taxi for Hogstein. We need them both out of there in five minutes. Watches in silent mode, please. Everybody ready?'

'Yes,' I said.

'Yep,' said the twins in freaky unison.

'*Si*,' said Camillo.

'*Da*,' said Anchka, to keep the international flavour.

Sniff, said Kirill.

And so it began.

Chapter 19

For all that planning, all that prep, the whole thing was over in one messy flash. Like a boxer who spends a whole year training, only to be slugged out cold in the first minute.

I lay and waited, shivering as snow trickled in from the hole above me. I heard Heidi and chums crashing around below. Wardrobes were shunted. Wallpaper torn. The fireplace bashed in. Jobs that were tailor-made for Pudders, the potato-faced wrecking ball. Kirill shone: instructing them where to shunt, where to tear, where to bash. He was specific but at the same time managed to sound reluctant. I heard what I presumed was a ladder get propped up close by. Heidi must have been in jewel-thief heaven.

'The Brillerge! Ooooh, the Brillerge! Mine, all mine, those lovely shiny toys just for me!'

The magic moment was approaching. But for some reason – whether it was the snowflake on my nose, or I'd caught Camillo's never-ending cold – that magic moment died.

I sneezed. A real sneeze, not a secret-code sneeze. I did try to hold it in. But it still made a noise like a tittering titmouse.

'What was that?' shrieked Heidi.

'Miss Heidi, I am sorry, but I have a cold,' I heard Kirill say. 'I did not mean to alarm you.'

'Ooh, it was *you*, was it, darling?? That's fishy. Because it certainly didn't come from your direction! Pudders!! Take a look outside!'

Get outta there, Anchka! Princess typed on our watches. **What the fluff, Anchovy?**

There was a painful wait as Pudders checked the corridor. I hoped he hadn't taken the sledgehammer.

Keep quiet next time! wrote Princess.

I'm sorry, was all I could reply.

Pudders returned. 'No one there,' he grumbled.

Good scramming, Anchka, I typed.

The spatula-keying was resumed. But now there was even more tension. Heidi had smelt something. Something other than Pudders' body odour. I heard the ladders creak as they climbed towards the key holes.

'Remember,' said Kirill to the gang, 'these keys only work if you turn them all at the same time. So, to help you, I will count to five, and you will all turn together. Okay?'

As quietly as I could, I slotted the spatula key in

place. It was crazy to think that Heidi, Justin and Pudders were only inches away, below the fake ceiling.

'One,' counted Kirill. 'Two. Three. Four. Fi-ATCHOOOOOOOOOOOO!!!'

It was a very convincing sneeze. The three bandits turned their spatula keys. I turned mine. And as I did, I heard the clamps in the vault let go of the casket, which squeaked and wailed inside the chimney, as a hundred years of grit hurtled out of the fireplace. All those noises were smothered by Heidi's demonic screech.

'NOOOOOOOOOOOOOOOOOOOOOO!!!!!!'

I was sucked back onto the rooftop. I rolled onto the snow and helped Camillo yank up the cable. Up came the casket. Gripping it like a limpet was a very sooty, and surprisingly heavy, Kirill. Black clouds puffed off him as we high-fived. Camillo covered the chimney to avoid them sending Justin up after us. For a few seconds we just lay on our backs panting, making accidental snow angels.

Got the casket! I typed to Princess.

Wooohooo!!

'Can we open it?' I said to Camillo and Kirill.

'Okay,' said Camillo. 'But only for a few minutes.'

After the elaborate effort to unlock all the keyholes, the casket was simple. It looked like an ordinary leather briefcase. But the contents were anything but ordinary. Nestled on blue velvet, four enamelled egg cups gleamed. They were mounted on little stands and sparkled with jewels in dazzling patterns. Even though he was covered in soot, I could see emotions dance across Kirill's face. Finally, they'd found them. The Brillerge egg cups. All those winter evenings he'd spent imagining them from his father's stories. Imagining how heavy they were, how they might reflect the light, how they might feel in his spindly hands. As we each held one, I saw all of Moscow around us: the kaleidoscopic churches, the starry spires, the columns of the Bolshoi, the floodlit statues, skyscrapers tiered like wedding cakes, and snow endlessly dancing in silvery spores. I'd never seen anything so beautiful.

'Hate to interrupt you kids,' said Princess on our watches. 'But faffing isn't an option.'

An excellent point very well made. Camillo fixed a cable to the edge of the roof.

'Yelena,' said Princess. 'What's happening with Hogstein's taxi?'

'Arriving any second now,' said Yelena.

Sure enough, I saw it below like a yellow toy car, pulling up by the foyer. And there, heaving with beef stroganoff, in his rumpled bonnet, was Mr Hogstein.

'Yaconda,' said Princess. 'Where's Swirly Ben?'

'Erm . . .' said Yaconda shakily. 'Slight problem. He went to the loo.'

'Please tell me it's a number one.'

'I didn't ask him, did I?'

'Aargh . . . Anchka, where are Heidi and the gang?'

'Sprinting down the stairs.'

Princess sighed. 'Anchovy, Kirill, Camillo, get off the roof.'

I was given the responsibility – or burden – of holding the casket. I was praying that Hogstein would step into the taxi and drive off. If he looked up and saw me, I could be in detention for, what? Ten years, minimum? But he was dawdling, looking as if he was waiting for something. I couldn't work out what.

Camillo lowered me down. I bumped into the building a few times. As I got lower, I heard the taxi's engine and the irate tapping of Hogstein's shoe. Why was he waiting? Why couldn't he just GET IN?!! The next few minutes were the 'messy flash' I mentioned earlier. One moment I was sliding down the hotel, held by a harness and Camillo and Kirill. The next, I was bouncing off a window with a horrible jerk, then treading air. The cable had snapped. The red carpet, the flags, the icy tarmac, the cars with their blacked-out windows, all wobbled before me. I closed my eyes. There was a *WHUMF* as I took a flagpole in the tender regions. Somehow, I wrapped my arms around this flagpole and clung to it like a long-lost brother. I didn't know which country's flag it was flying. But I did know this: I had dropped the casket. It's hard to know which sight was worse. The gruesome outline of Justin above, holding a pair of pliers. Or the casket, upright in the snow, right beside Hogstein.

Perhaps worst of all was the way he said, 'Ah,

there it is,' as he picked it up.

'Let me help you with your briefcase, sir,' said
the driver helpfully as he loaded up the casket
and Hog, then got in and revved his engine.
Unkle Pudders came charging out, moving with
surprising athleticism for someone so potato-
shaped.

'STOP!!' he roared in that ear-splitting crackle.

But clearly, Hogstein didn't want to miss
his flight. Nor his starring role in our school
production.

The taxi sped off.

Chapter 20

I looked up at Justin, who was reaching for something much nastier than pliers. Once again, the superpower of fear kicked in. With a sudden Hulk-like strength, I rose on my flagpole, gripped the railings on the balcony above, and chin-upped a level. Still in Hulk-mode, I ripped open the window and toppled in. This wasn't a catering room – that would've been too convenient. It was a bedroom. I dashed through as a shouty man – I *think* he had forgotten to put his pyjamas and pants on – shook a fist at me with one hand and held a cushion over his modesty with the other. Outside, I flew through the corridors, searching for the kitchen and fellow G.S.L.-ers.

'You alive, Anchovy?!' said Princess on the pizza watch.

'Just,' I whispered. 'It was that dirty weasel Justin, he cut my –'

'I know, I know, Anchovy. It's a complete shish-up. Twins, where are you?'

'We're in the reading room, still.'

'What do you mean, still? Has Swirly Ben got the runs?'

'No, he's here,' whispered Yelena – or Yaconda. 'But we can't talk right now.'

They transferred to text.

What's the situ? P.S.

Not great. Y+Y

Anchovy, Anchka, get along there, but stay hidden, okay?

I eventually found the kitchen, where Anchka was waiting. She put her hand on what looked like a spice rack and opened a trapdoor. We squeezed in and crawled along a passage. After five minutes, she turned and put a finger to her lips, then pointed at a peephole. It showed a mustard-yellow room with log fire crackling, old, dark bookshelves and grape-green chairs. In one sat Swirly Ben, with a shaking newspaper. The twins were either side of him. Facing them, if I looked down far enough, was Justin. He was holding something very black and very shiny and very gun-shaped.

'Oh, Heidi!' he bawled. 'Unkle Puuuuuuudders! Look who I've found!!'

Heidi strode in, the fire-glow making her face look like a Halloween pumpkin.

'Now then, Swirly Ben!' snapped Justin, getting cocky. 'Time to hand over that case you just pinched.'

Swirly Ben looked really, really confused. He might have forgotten where he was. Or who he was. His pink-tinged eyes quivered behind the lenses. He remained silent.

'You know what I mean!' jeered Justin and swiped the newspaper aside, revealing a leather briefcase on Swirly Ben's lap. Its shape and size were worryingly familiar.

'Open it up, Swirly Ben . . .' Justin actually had the bad taste to prod the poor guy in the shin. 'Or else.'

Swirly Ben blinked rapidly and opened his mouth. I knew what was coming. Some riddle or poem. All I had ever heard him say was gibberish. But I was wrong. So wrong.

'My name, young man,' he said, with a devilish smoothness, 'is Arnold Hogstein. I am a retired history professor . . .' (Professor? Note the upgrade.) 'and I am – or should I say *was* – enjoying my first visit to this beautiful city on holiday with my granddaughters.' He gestured at the twins. 'That is, until you accosted me with what appears to be a water pistol. I believe, my child, you are gravely mistaken.'

'Nice try, Benny Boy,' sneered the revolting Juice Box. 'But you're still not opening that case, are you? And trust me, it isn't water inside this bad-boy.'

Why did he talk like that? So lame.

Swirly Ben gave a wonderfully mocking chuckle. Now I saw all. Hogstein had taken the casket. Swirly Ben had taken Hogstein's briefcase. And he was stalling these thugs while the Brillerge got away.

'Well, my dear boy, of course I am only too glad to open my case for you.' He swung it open. 'As you can see, this is my . . . er . . .'

I could see he was improvising now and hadn't

bargained for the mad tat Hogstein would be carrying. 'Yes, this is my, er, my guide to the antique chamber pots of the Kremlin . . . and here is my um . . . my underwear. I do . . .' The old boy cleared his throat and went on with admirable fighting spirit. 'I do, er, prefer to have my underwear on the *brief* side, shall we say. And yes, that tube you're holding, young man, that, erm . . .'

'It says "cream for piles" on it,' said Justin, stunned. 'Piles of what?'

'That is a personal matter,' said Swirly Ben, coming into the home strait. 'Was there something in my briefcase you wished to find, young man? Have I mistakenly taken something of yours? A teddy, perhaps?'

Justin was silent.

'What is the *meaning* of this, Justin?' screamed Heidi.

Unkle Pudders thundered in.

'Miss Heidi, Miss Heidi,' he wheezed. 'Swirly Ben's got away in a taxi.'

'But THIS is Swirly Ben!' wailed Justin, distraught. 'I KNOW it's him. I know these girls! They're not his granddaughters!'

Pudders looked like he wanted to drop-kick Justin out of the window. He wasn't the only one.

'Listen, lad, while you're wasting our time, the real Swirly Ben is heading to the airport with some bloomin' expensive egg cups. I saw him on the train and I saw him leave the hotel. So how about you –'

'Yes!' weighed in Heidi. 'You stupid little squirt! Swirly Ben is GETTING AWAY! And you're trying to take some credit by dragging in this delirious old codger!'

'Who are you calling a delicious old badger, my dear?' croaked Swirly Ben, perhaps overdoing it. Heidi huffed, lugged at Glitterpuff's lead, and the gang hopped it. Justin was throwing the mother of all hissy fits.

Swirly Ben frowned after them, picked up the newspaper and began filling in the crossword. I marvelled at the ancient detective: 108 years old. Still got it.

Chapter 21

e listened to the whirr of the G.S.L. shuttle as it surfaced in the Metropole's fake freezer. Anchka slid open the panel. We helped Lyosha out of the first carriage and Mr Kitov out of the second. He was doubled up like a deckchair. He blinked at his surroundings before spotting his soot-covered son. Sobbing, he folded him in his gangly arms. He patted down Kirill, which made him equally sooty, as the flow of 'what-where-how-why' poured between them. Anchka translated.

'Mr Kitov is saying how there was an extremely

nasty little boy who hit him on the head and held him captive in the theatre.'

Kirill was nodding, tears painting lines on his sooty face.

'Apparently,' said Anchka, 'Mr Kitov refused to talk about the spatula necklace. But they went to hunt Kirill down anyway.'

'Don't worry,' I said between gritted teeth. 'That sick little Juice Box has got it coming.'

'On that note, Anchovy,' said Princess, 'I suggest you get in that freezer and lie on the fake prawns. Anchka, I'm guessing you guys have an airport shuttle, right?'

Anchka nodded. That was my last sight of her – she closed the door and released me along the rails at breakneck speed to the airport. I now had to stop a gang of homicidal jewellery thieves from topping off my history teacher. Camillo got hacking, pulling whatever strings he could

to whizz me through security. At Domodedovo
Airport, delegates at various food stalls – pancake
cafés, dumpling bars, sweet shops – took me
along shortcuts, passing me information on the
way. Yes, they'd seen the gang, tearing through
security. Yes, they had delayed them as much as
they could. Justin had been particularly whiny over
the chocolate souvenirs in the departures lounge.
The good news: Hogstein had already taken off for
London, on the 17:35. The bad news: Heidi and
co. weren't far behind, on the 18:45. I'd be on this
flight too, stashed at the back near the cabin crew.
As we drew closer, I was ordered to the toilet. The
Hoverbog. Again.

'We'll parachute you in over Rufflington,' said
Princess. 'Head straight to school and swipe the
casket when Hogstein goes on stage.'

I couldn't decide if travelling by Hoverbog was
worse as a shocking surprise or with the long dread

of anticipation. At about seven o'clock UK time, I was on the loo seat, helmeted, goggled, seatbelted, and ready to pump the fake soap dispenser. (I even used the toilet, since I was there.) Everything was ready. Except the lock on the door. Why must I always fluff up the basics? As it rattled, I knew who would barge in. A snarling Justin. As I had one hand on the soap dispenser, another pulling up my pants, I had to just kick out at him. He dodged and charged at my head.

'Why's it always YOU, pizza-face?' he hollered. 'Why won't you just GO AWAY?'

The feeling was mutual. He was clawing so wildly, and I was ducking so rapidly, that we were both just doing stupid things like me hitting my head on the sink and Justin's fist snapping off the flush button instead of snapping off my head. That's the thing with fights. They're never cool. In films, they're slick and stylish. But in real life it's just clumsy-looking goons swiping at thin air, tripping on toilet rolls and banging their chin on a septic tank. I took a scurry of little punches before kneeing him off. I pumped the soap dispenser for all I was worth. The horrible *whoosh* bellowed around us. Justin covered his ears. I was shot out of the plane. I saw Justin framed in the hatch like a postage stamp, his angry pug-face watching me disappear. Again the icy clouds. Again the wobbling horizon. Again the giddying patchwork of fields and farms. Sparks were shooting from the Hoverbog. It began to shake violently.

'Princessssssssssss!' I shouted over the pizza watch. 'The Hoverbog's malfunctioning!'

Justin must've ripped out some vital part during our scrap.

'Hold tight, Anch,' shouted Princess. 'We've got your back! Camillo's bringing you in to land . . .'

There was a deafening *POP* and the twilit

rectangles of Rufflington Community School swam into view. My parachute was sparking and burning as I spiralled towards the football pitches. Their white lines seemed to float, criss-crossing in mid-air, barging into each other. My stomach lurched. I don't remember landing.

I can't say how long I lay in the mud, or what woke me. Perhaps it was the gurgling of the pizza watch. Or perhaps the wall of fire. It had scorched the goalposts, where a piece of the Hoverbog had fallen off – the engine? – and exploded in the nets. I lay in the centre circle, wrapped in my parachute/death shroud. The flames were advancing. For a second I thought I'd died and gone to hell because, standing above me in a red tracksuit, lacking just the pitchfork and horns, was Mr Brewster, gawping at the apocalypse. What had once been his sacred football pitch now resembled the Battle of Passchendaele.

'What have you done, Colin?!!' he yelled. 'We're supposed to be playing Nuttingville High School in the semi-final tomorrow!'

PE teachers. No perspective sometimes.

'This is . . . this is –'

Before he could say 'unbelievable' or 'unacceptable' or 'grounds for expelling you',

he rolled his eyes, swayed and *WHUMFFED* down in the mud. A tiny blue dart was stuck in his rump. 'It's just a mild tranquiliser,' said a tall silhouette with a hook-shaped ponytail. 'He'll wake up in two minutes, so we need to get going. Are you okay?'

I wiped the sludge off my face.

'Just about, Princess.'

As we jogged towards the school, she broke
the bad news. Somehow – they may have crash-
landed the plane, they may have had parachutes –
but Heidi and co. were *already here*, heading up
the school drive. The sports hall – which doubled
as the theatre – was at the back. We had time to
sneak in, take the Brillerge, and lock Hogstein in
the equipment room – if he hadn't gone on stage.
We hid in the bike sheds and peered towards
the gates. A pigtailed beanpole was snaking up
the drive. Princess took out her blow-pipe and
loaded up more darts. Hopefully they weren't
mere tranquillisers. She handed me a new molten-
tomato-purée gun.

'We need to split. There's a ton of people in
the front entrance, so take the back doors, get the

casket, and for pitta's sake *don't* let Hogstein on the stage.'

Sound advice for life in general.

'What about you? Are you tackling Heidi on your own?'

'I can take her. And no, the police and fire brigade will be here shortly. Now get going before Glitterpuff smells you!'

I sprinted behind the sports hall. Since Mr Brewster was crawling into the changing rooms, I had to go via the equipment room, which opened out behind the stage. The double doors were easy – Camillo could fiddle with the alarm system – but the doors to backstage were locked from inside. Through the frosted glass panels came the muffled drone of Hogstein. I had to admire him – a flight from Russia and straight to the school play. The man was dedicated, if a bit bonkers. He would surely go turbo-bonkers at my next move. In my defence, I hadn't even touched my G.S.L. *Elementary Lock-picking Manual*. So I only really had one option. I grabbed a hockey stick, smashed the glass, and stuck my arm through for the bolt. Once in, I faced the stage curtains. Horrified prefects loitered in the wings, ready to wheel on some naff cardboard background. On a stool was Hogstein's coat and bonnet. Next to it was the casket. But no Hogstein. He *was* on the stage. The pizza watch beeped.

I took down the wolf and Pudders but the police STILL aren't here. HHH is in the building. I'm coming but just FYI.

Hardly surprising about Rufflington police. Their work in this yawnsville was mostly telling pensioners where they could or couldn't park their mobility scooters. News that a maniac like Heidi was at large would probably cause a meltdown. Behind the curtain, the audience was quiet.

Hogstein was in the middle of some long, rambling speech.

Princess messaged:

Have you got Hogstein?

Almost.

Grabbing the casket, I stared at the curtains and took a deep breath. Hogstein's waffling was reaching a climax. It was probably very poignant. Then again, he might also have the red dot of a sniper dancing over his dome. Perhaps the play actually needed a bit of spicing up. I stepped through the curtains. The audience sat up as if they'd been electrocuted.

Rocking a vile pair of breeches and a lacy blouse with a vomit-inducing neckline, Hogstein turned and gave me his nastiest look to date. His jaw resembled a ventriloquist's dummy's. His eyebrows threatened to evacuate his head. His hacking, spluttering death rattle pierced the air.

'K-K-K-Kingsley . . .'

'Get off the stage, sir.'

His cheeks rippled like flabby whirlpools.

'Boyyyy! BOYYYY!'

'Please, sir. Please get off the stage. You'll be killed if you don't.'

He stared at the hockey stick in my hands.

Then Dexter's laddy voice rang out.

'Sir, sir, the football pitch is on fire, sir!'

The audience gasped as one.

Hogstein stared at my charred trench coat and face. The hockey stick again. A wild glint lit behind his glasses. He was picturing the houseboat. The fire alarm in Rome. He was putting two and two together. And making minus five.

'Kingsley,' he spluttered again. 'You're *insane*.'

On this bombshell – well, not actual bombshell, that was to come a few minutes later – the lights went out. The voices of a thousand parents exploded in clucking alarm.

Then, among the darkness, high up near the ceiling, a small rectangle of yellow light slapped itself on our retinas. The lighting and sound booth. Inside was a silhouette, spiky and lean. With pigtails.

'What have you *done*, Kingsley?' Hogstein hissed.

The voice of Heidi Hyde High came on the loudspeaker, turning my blood to ice-cold slush.

'Ladies and gentlemen, boys and girls. This is an important announcement.'

'Who the *dickens* is that woman, Kingsley?' Hogstein bayed. 'I certainly didn't see her among the board of governors! I demand an ex–'

'The man on the stage,' cooed Heidi Hyde High frostily, 'is a thief and a fraud. And that boy is his accomplice.'

The audience exploded into another cluck-fest.

'Well, I mean to say!' shouted Hogstein, advancing to the front of the stage. 'Who on earth do you think you are?'

The silhouette paused before uttering the fateful words, 'Your executioner, Swirly Ben.'

The clucks turned to screams. Chairs were scraping. Stilettoes a-moving.

'Swirly Bun?' I heard Hogstein mutter. The old boy could still think about food at a time like this. There wasn't time to think about baked goods, though, because another rectangle of light appeared. Framed within it, clutching something small and metallic, was the dumpy little form of Justin.

'From Rufflington with love,' he sneered before sliding the object down the aisle, where it bumped against the stage and came to a halt.

'What is that?' gurgled Hogstein.

It was a tin of caviar. And of course, you didn't

have to be a rocket scientist to guess what a tin of caviar from HHH meant. I calculated that we had about four seconds before the inevitable explosion of poisonous gas. A blur of animal instinct took over me. The tin. The hockey stick. The rectangle in the distance. I hadn't even thought, *Right, I'm going to swing this stick and tonk this tin*. My arms got the memo before my brain even sent it. The following images still stick in my mind:

Me, leaning back, the hockey stick arcing above my head. What few muscles I had tightening with the returning **SNAP**. Stick against tin. Tin against air. Tin sailing past ceiling. Tin against yellow rectangle. Yellow rectangle shattering into a riot of glass and gas. Hogstein shouting, '*HOOOOOOLIGAN!*' (which was really ungrateful, considering I had just saved his life). Hogstein passing out in shock. The orchestra abandoning their instruments.

The audience ran for the stage, the doors, the windows, their jumpers and scarfs muffling their faces, but not really their screams. Princess was trying to swim through them like a salmon trying to get upstream. She ran through the chairs towards me and the heap of Hogstein. She grabbed his ankles and I tucked my arms under his pits. It was the second time in a week I'd had to lug this guy. We staggered through the melee, as police sirens wailed in the distance. Perhaps they'd finally found their truncheons. But way louder than any siren came the last wail of the pigtailed demon.

'STOP, YOU INSOLENT LITTLE WRETCH!'

I say 'pigtailed', but when she emerged from the shattered lighting and sound booth, I saw that her hair had exploded into a fuzzy tornado. Her smashed sunglasses hung askew. Her tan-line panda eyes manically popped. She grabbed a gym rope. And then she swung down towards us, a

screaming, fuming, fur-coated Tarzan. I swung the hockey stick and connected, but at the same time, something connected with me – her high-heeled boot, clonking me on the jaw. The casket went flying. Hogstein slumped to the floor. Princess dragged him by his breeches through the carnage of chairs. Heidi lashed at me with something suspiciously resembling a sword. It missed me and ploughed through a chair leg. It looked suspiciously like a sword because it *was* a sword. Trust Hogstein to actually care about sourcing authentic props. Backing off, I raised the hockey stick, parrying her lightning chops. On and on she swiped, screaming at me, and further back I went, towards the climbing equipment and the cricket nets.

'You HORRIBLE' – swipe; another chair mutilated – 'LITTLE' – swipe; a music stand scattered – 'DEVIOUS' – swipe – 'FILTHY' – swipe – 'VERMINOUS' – swipe –

'TREACHEROUS' – swipe – 'DISGUSTING' – swipe – 'BOY! YOU WILL PAY FOR THIS! YOU WILL PAY FOR MESSING WITH HEIDI HYDE HIGH!!!' – swipe swipe swipe.

'Anchovy!' cried Princess.

I had run out of space. I was trying to climb onto a gym horse when another slash took a chunk out of my mum's trench coat (I'd definitely need to buy her a new one) and pranged me in the butt cheek. I rolled off the gym horse and knocked my head on a bench. Fumbling, I raised the purée gun but Heidi read my mind, lashing out and sending the gun into orbit. Her sword flashed above me. As I gazed at Heidi's triumphant orange face, framed by her mad-scientist hair, everything went quiet.

Out of the corner of my eye, I caught a glimpse of something falling. Something silky and vast. It was the cricket nets, cascading in slow motion. Someone at the highest rung of the climbing wall was hacking them off with a pair of scissors. As they fell, they enveloped Heidi Hyde High, swallowing her up like a fly in a web.

'AAAAAARGGHHHHHHHHH!!!!!! YOU LITTLE TERRORS! YOU LITTLE BRATS! YOU SCOUNDRELS!! YOU! YOU! YOU!' She was practically hiccupping with insults.

'Grab a corner, Princess!' I shouted.

We circled Heidi again and again, bundling her up, tighter and tighter, like an Egyptian mummy, until she toppled, defeated. It was at this moment, when they had literally *no* work left to do, that Rufflington police force bumbled into the sports hall. I slumped against the ladders and stared up at where the cricket nets once hung. Scuttling across as nimble as a squirrel, clutching scissors, with absolutely no regard for health and safety, was Alicia.

'Good work, bro!' she grinned.

My little sister had saved the day.

Chapter 22

I gave her the biggest hug ever. Her blonde head nestled in my shoulder, her wonky fringe tickling my chin. Alicia had defeated Heidi Hyde High.

'Allie, how did you know . . .'

'Well, seeing you in Mum's trench coat falling from the sky on a toilet did worry me a little. I headed to the school and took it from there.'

'I expect you'll be wanting more than just truck-loads of fruit pastilles now . . .'

'Col, I was joking! You almost actually died. Don't worry about the fruit pastilles. Well, a packet would be nice . . .'

By the ambulance, a paramedic was asking Hogstein how many fingers they were holding up.

'Are you okay, sir?' I asked cautiously. I didn't want to make him burst a vein just by seeing me. He looked perplexed. He wore a look that seemed to say, *now I've seen everything. Literally everything.*

'I'm really sorry, sir, honestly, about what happened. I was only trying to –'

'I think I'm beginning to see, Kingsley . . .' He shook his head.

'Sir, I just . . . if I hadn't run away from you, and if I hadn't pushed you out of that moving train . . . and if I hadn't gatecrashed your play and smashed the door plus the lighting and sound booth and set fire to the football pitch . . . Well, sir, I'm not just saying this . . . but you would've been *killed.*'

'Maybe.' He rubbed his chin. 'Maybe,

Kingsley . . . well. I don't know what to think any more. There's more to you than meets the eye. You're not simply a truant-playing pyromaniac. But . . .' A rare look of sympathy came into his eyes. 'I doubt the headteacher will believe you.'

The paramedics resumed their prodding.

'Oh Kingsley,' called Hogstein as we made to leave. 'I don't know why I'm bothering to ask this, but did you at least fill in any of the worksheets?'

From my pocket, I fished out the charred, mud-stained remains of my homework. Judging by the look Hogstein gave them, they might as well have been scraps of toilet paper. He sighed deeply and waved us away. Alicia and I left him, and headed through the crowds of police, firemen, teachers and panicking parents. Apparently ours would be here any minute. I felt an elbow in my ribs.

'Your GF is here.' Alicia smirked.

'She's not my – oh, hi Princess.'

'*Princess*? That is *so* your GF name for your GF.'

'You must be Alicia,' said Princess Skewer, towering above her in her long pinstriped coat and massive trainers. 'I think we spoke on the phone.'

'Yeah,' said Alicia, frowning. 'You've got some *terrible* language on you, Princess.'

'I like your cheek.'

'I say it like I see it.'

'No, I'm being serious,' said Princess, looking around furtively. 'I genuinely like it.' She passed Alicia a little blue calling card. 'We could use someone like you.'

Alicia squinted at the card, and looked back at Princess, clearly not fully trusting her.

'Are you a burglar?'

Princess laughed. 'Ask your brother.' She spotted my parents and turned to go. '*Dosvidanya,*

Anchovy. And congrats. The Brillerge egg cups will be back where they belong.' She tucked the casket under her arm and slunk off.

'Alicia!' squealed my mum. 'Colin! We were *so* worried about you both!'

She squished us into a hug tighter than the clamps on the Brillerge vault.

As our old Volvo spluttered back to Caesar Pizza, Alicia and I faced a barrage of questions. Some we had to dodge, some we had to fudge. Yes, there had been some problems in Russia, but nothing major, and the host family were very, very nice. Yes, there had been a kerfuffle at the school play. Well, we think it was probably some deranged school governor. Yes, she was sort of wielding a sword. Yes, we were the last people in the hall and so we did get tangled up in it a bit. Yes, we're fine. No, we can't remember how the trench coat got so wrecked. No, we didn't realise there was a tranquillised wolf on the school drive. No, we're not part of any secret organisation and have no knowledge of what this is about or why there was an assassination attempt on Mr Hogstein and what was so special about his briefcase. Yes, we would love some anchovy pizza.

We entered the pizzeria. Our mascot Markus Anchovius seemed to wink at me. Or perhaps it was just a trick of the moonlight.

'Mind the wet floor,' grumbled our dad.

'It's all very mysterious,' sighed our mum, getting out the rolling pin.

'Very mysterious,' added our dad, taking out the toppings.

Alicia and I sat at the brand-spanking-new marble counter – made possible by the generous donation of a mystery customer, which had enabled my parents to give Caesar Pizza a much-needed facelift. For mystery customer, read:

G.S.L. salary. (I couldn't keep it all; that would be greedy.) The cheesy, salty-fishy waft of a cooked Mark Anchovy pizza filled the room.

'So,' said Alicia, taking out Princess's card. 'When do I start?'